To Karen

COME AUGUST,
COME FREEDOM

COME AUGUST, COME FREEDOM

The Bellows, the Gallows, and the Black General Gabriel

GIGI AMATEAU

CANDLEWICK PRESS

Copyright © 2012 by Gigi Amateau

First paperback edition 2014

The Library of Congress has cataloged the hardcover edition as follows:

Amateau, Gigi, date.
Come August, come freedom : the bellows, the gallows, and the black general Gabriel / Gigi Amateau. — 1st ed.
p. cm.
Summary: Imagines the childhood and youth of "Prosser's Gabriel," a courageous and intelligent blacksmith in post-Revolutionary Richmond, Virginia, who roused thousands of African-Americans slaves like himself to rebel.
ISBN 978-0-7636-4792-6 (hardcover)
1. Prosser, Gabriel, ca. 1775–1800 — Juvenile fiction.
[1. Prosser, Gabriel, ca. 1775–1800 — Fiction.
2. Slavery — Fiction. 3. African Americans — Virginia — Fiction.
4. Slave insurrections — Fiction.
5. Virginia — History — 1775–1865 — Fiction.]   I. Title.
PZ7.A49157Com   2012
[Fic] — dc23   2011048342

ISBN 978-0-7636-6870-9 (paperback)

13 14 15 16 17 18 BVG 10 9 8 7 6 5 4 3 2 1

Printed in Berryville, VA, U.S.A.

This book was typeset in Caslon 540.

Candlewick Press
99 Dover Street
Somerville, Massachusetts 02144

visit us at www.candlewick.com

Dare you see a Soul at the White Heat?
Then crouch within the door.

—EMILY DICKINSON

CHAPTER ONE
March 1777

MA BELIEVED. One Sunday before sunrise, she headed out early for church at Young's spring with her infant, Gabriel, swaddled and slung across her chest. She walked briskly along the footpath that she and so many others before had worn to the creek. Later, Pa would join them for worship, bringing the oldest boy, Martin, while toting the middle one, Solomon.

Since Gabriel's birth, Ma kept most of her days at the great house; away from the field, which she was glad to be, but away from her husband, which left her empty. The cook, Kissey, often reminded her to give thanks for Mrs. Prosser, who granted Ma a weekly

Sunday reunion, but Ma yearned for more than half a borrowed morning with her family.

Ma did give thanks for her friends. "Praise the Lord for Kissey and Old Major," Ma said aloud now as she set her baby down.

In her pocket nestled the apple seeds; she had kept them safe and deep in her apron until the captive ground of winter gave way to spring's rightful thaw. The morning smelled of sunshine, new grass, and flowers to come. Before she reached the stream where all the people from all the quarters would gather to pray, Ma squatted down on the still side of the hill. There at the south end of Brookfield plantation, she tugged, and the reluctant earth opened enough for her to place the seeds.

She could hear the tinkle of the creek beyond the field. *When the rain comes, before long, that trickle will be a roar,* she thought.

Gabriel began to root around for his second meal of the day, and Ma could not help but think of the other hungry babe. Brookfield's infant master, little Thomas Henry Prosser, would need to eat soon, too. The missus could produce no milk of her own, so Ma fed both boys.

For times when Ma would be away from the great

house, Old Major had fashioned a wooden spout from persimmon wood so that Kissey could feed Thomas Henry the early milk Ma squeezed from herself. If that milk ran out and the little master turned fussy, Kissey would placate him with a sugar teat until Ma returned. The missus rarely asked for her son before noon on Sundays, anyway.

Praise the Lord for Ann Prosser's Sunday sick headaches. Ma gave thanks for this, too. She stretched out long in the grass and nursed her six-month-old son without interruption. After while, Gabriel opened his walnut eyes, and Ma gave him her other breast. On some Sundays, he got his fair share.

Ma stroked Gabriel's troubled brow. "Eat all you like, child. Take what's yours."

When he finished, Gabriel protested being wrapped up so tight. He pushed away from Ma with his head, the only part of him unhemmed and unbound. Kissey had warned her not to loosen his dressing; the crude March air might do the child harm.

Ma unswaddled her son. "Another baby'd fall fast asleep from such a full little belly. You wide awake, my Gabriel."

She swept him up and then swung him down— from the earth to the dawning sky and back. When his tender bare feet brushed along the downy grass, the baby laughed. He tried to stand on his own, and Ma approved. "Oh-ho! Where you off to, my strappin' boy? You got business at the market, work in the city? My baby boy off to the sea?"

What Ma believed was this: her youngest son would grow strong and grow free. He would run pick an apple anytime he pleased, even if only to taste the good fruit given by the Lord, and see, from this spot, the amber sunrise painted by His hand.

She reflected on the talk so often heard in the quarter and the stories Pa brought back from the city, stories of a people insisting on freedom. *Tall tales*, she had first thought. *Tall tales of a David thinkin' to slay a giant.* Yet Pa had been right all along. Virginia and the other colonies had condemned rule by tyranny and were now at war with England.

Ma prayed aloud for the apple seeds and for Gabriel, her youngest-born. "Lord, set my Gabriel free, too. One way or another, set my angel-boy free." She kissed the baby in the hollow of his tender neck and refused to bind him up again.

The Lord sent a gentle rain that same afternoon and a blessed sunshine the next morning. From the soil once full enough to grow tobacco, now completely spent, God and Ma together helped the apple tree's roots grow deep and its limbs slowly full on the protected shelf in the hill overlooking the spring. Gabriel grew, too.

CHAPTER TWO
March 1786

GABRIEL LIVED with his mother and his two brothers in a small hut at the edge of the woods, just up the hill from the creek, only a short ways from the swamp, and a fair enough distance from the great house. Their home's only window served also as the doorway to one room, where they cooked and ate, where they prayed and slept.

A hole in the ground held an ever-burning fire for cooking, warming, and keeping away bugs. A second hole, knocked in the wall, drew the smoke out. Beside the fire hole stood a table made by Pa, and at the east end of the room, a bed of Pa's hand, too. To make it, Pa had felled a black-walnut tree, stripped the bark, smoothed the boards, and turned the posts.

Ma had delivered Gabriel in that bed, with Pa at her side. Even under threat of a well-laid-on lashing, Pa had not left his wife in her time. And when Gabriel entered the world, Pa breathed on the boy first.

Nowdays, Ma slept alone on the mattress pieced from coarse, heavy Negro cloth and piled with corn husks. Martin, Solomon, and Gabriel slept on the floor—Gabriel right at the door. So that the breeze would cool his skin, on hot nights he slept atop a wool rug, issued him by Mr. Prosser. In cold weather, Gabriel curled up beneath his rug and tried to keep warm. And by full-moon light, Gabriel could see well enough to memorize words from the book given him by Mrs. Prosser. He liked his sleeping spot; from this place Gabriel could see and hear everything in the night.

Whenever Old Major, who lived just across the yard, got up to grind his weekly corn ration with the hand mill that all the folks shared, Gabriel knew Ma's turn would come next. Every time, Old Major's hound dog let Gabriel know when to rouse Ma. Whether Dog counted up the minutes or whether she detected the slightest finishing-up shift in Old Major's weight, Gabriel did not know. But whenever Ma's turn came, Dog always gave a half howl, and Gabriel would then wake his ma. Soon after the little yowl, Old Major and Dog would appear in the yard between the huts.

Last summer was when Dog had first come to them, snarling and growling, seeking refuge in the quarter. At first, the year-old pup had acted more like a rattlesnake than a hound. The women and children hid from her; the men tried to beat and subdue her — all except Old Major, who said to the insolent beast, "Keep still; you all right. Set down here. I know just how you feel." And soon after, Dog let the people in the quarter come to know her.

Old Major would only call her Dog. The quiet man's own given name had been put away since ever Gabriel could remember. Ma said a dash toward freedom was what got the master started on saying "Old Major." Ma said Old Major's run happened before Gabriel was born.

According to the women, Old Major had changed since being hunted down and dragged back to Brookfield. Even Gabriel knew the story of how Prosser's man had tied the captured freedom fighter to a tree and hit him with a tobacco stick until Old Major's true spirit left him and took up in the ebony heartwood of the persimmon to which he was bound.

ADVERTISEMENT *Virginia Gazette*

HENRICO COUNTY, NOV. 2, 1775

Ran away last Night, a Negro Man named James, who is a very shrewd sensible Fellow, and can both read and write; and he always waited upon me, he must be well known throughout most of Virginia. He is very brown, about 5 Feet 9 Inches high, marked with the Smallpox, is very fond of going into the Water. He took a Variety of Clothes, stole several of my shirts, a saddle bag and my light Bay Mare, about 3 Years old. From the Circumstances, there is Reason to believe he intends an Attempt to get to Lord Dunmore. His Elopement was from no Cause of Complaint, or Dread of a Whipping (for he has always been remarkably indulged, indeed too much so) but from a determined Resolution to get Liberty, as he conceived by flying to Lord Dunmore. I will give 5L to any Person who secures him and the Mare, so that I get them again.

Even when the night was still, such olden memories lived on in the quarter, keeping Gabriel awake.

On some rare Saturday nights, he would listen to Old Major playing the fiddle and calling a dance in the forest, right below the quarter. He could hear Kissey's spoons, too, holding the rhythm of every tune. When the two of them got going strong, the neighbor kin would holler out, "Go on! Go on!" Often, an old voice Gabriel recognized but could not place would shout above the music and the laughter, "Shine it up! Shine out!"

Sometimes the slowest mournful ballad would fill Gabriel with delight. Sometimes a fast jig could make him cry. And sometimes a piece that was supposed to sound happy and content could draw out moaning and wailing from the very earth, from the trees, the creek — as if all the peoples' sufferings were alive and lingering there in the notes, as if all the people were calling out *Come, freedom. Come, freedom. Freedom, go on and come.* Those times, Gabriel knew in his heart that the familiar voice he heard was Old Major's true spirit, now binding to the dance from the deep, black heart of the persimmon. He wondered whether everyone else heard it, too.

On these nights, when the grown folks made

music and dancing together—when they practiced at joy—Gabriel suspected that every chestnut and cedar, hickory and oak, in the night forest united to sway and rock the people into a little place of happiness to help them bear another day. He loved nothing so much as to fall asleep tapping his feet to the sounds of his beautiful people, safe in the dark woods.

He had once overheard Mrs. Prosser laughing with another missus. "Virginians would rather die than not dance!" From his place by the door, he could tell she was right: dancing was a dangerous pastime for his people, but even so, they would not stop.

On occasion the fierce urgency of his kin's dancing seemed to rise up out of the woods, insistent on reaching the great house. Now and then, through a cracked window, an open flue, or the propped-wide kitchen door, the people's singing even breached Mr. Prosser's dreams and woke him. *Come, freedom. Come, freedom. Freedom, go on and come.* On those dangerous nights, the trees could not protect the people. The whole forest could not help.

When the fiddle turned suddenly silent and the lively sounds of the dance fell hush, Gabriel knew that Prosser's man was coming down. On those nights, he would suspend his breath and pray Ma's psalms while the people slipped off into the shadows and melted away into the trees. During the eerie quiet, Gabriel would stay awake until he heard all return, and until he didn't hear the shot of a gun.

Ma never went to dances anymore, not since Prosser's man took Pa off to Richmond. Prosser's man had come back to Brookfield with the cart full of new people from the city, packed with fine goods from the market house, but empty of Pa. At first, after Pa and his stories of freedom vanished, Ma took to the bed built by her husband.

From his place by the door, Gabriel watched his mother weeping. At night Ma cried, "Tell me, why would the Lord take my husband? What can a woman do, Lord? Tell me."

Ma seemed deaf to Solomon's tears and blind to Martin's retreat into himself. She would not rise even to grind corn. When her turn came around, Gabriel went instead, and Dog went with him. At the mill, with no one to see but Dog, Gabriel wept, too.

Like Pa and for Pa, Ma resisted what life Brookfield had to offer her. After a short little while of Ma's absence from the field, Gabriel saw Prosser's man crossing the yard toward their hut.

"Ma?" Gabriel had said. "Somebody's coming."

Gabriel's mother had curled up tight against Pa's bedpost. But the man picked her up and hauled her to the woodshed next to the tobacco barn. Solomon could not stop him, and Martin dared not try. All three brothers pretended still to sleep when Ma staggered back to the quarter with her white slip in bloody shreds.

The smell of Ma's torn flesh filled up their hut—a reminder that theirs was a family always at the mercy. Martin and Solomon could not stand to be near her. For a while, they slept elsewhere. Martin, who at the age of eighteen often found reasons to leave the quarter, took to the forest. Ten-year-old Solomon went to stay with Kissey.

Gabriel remained in his place on the floor, but he hardly slept for keeping watch over Ma. During the day, he went with his mother instead of to the great house for his lessons with Thomas Henry. *From here on*, he thought, *I'll keep Ma from all danger.*

After the beating, Ma returned to the field where the people trudged through the tobacco, digging up cutworms and plucking away hornworms. Kissey came at night to doctor her up and to show Gabriel how to

wash the gashes in his mother's back with a tincture
of apple-cider vinegar and herbs from the kitchen garden. To Gabriel, Ma's whip marks resembled the earth
between the tobacco hills, newly tilled and ready for
planting.

CHAPTER THREE
July 1786

Thomas Prosser Daily Journal—
Brookfield 1786

Monday, July 10—Very hot day. No breeze.
Mrs. Prosser unwell. The medicine Kissey
gave made her sicker. All hands grubbing.

Tuesday, July 11—Hot day. Unbearable to go
to town. Mrs. Prosser still suffering. Sent
Old Major to town to pick up furniture.
Hands still grubbing.

Wednesday, July 12—Very hot day. Like
August, only worse. Mrs. Prosser much
better this morning. Hands grubbing.

GABRIEL COULD SEE how Ma feared to ease up in the field after the whipping. He was still too young then to be made to work all day in the 'baccy, but he took to walking alongside his ma—helping her—so that she would not fall farther behind.

Pa had left Ma in the family way, but despite her imminent condition, she had to labor alongside the other women to save the crop from the ravenous hornworms. Crooked and bent between the tobacco, Ma turned over the thousands of leaves on the hundreds of plants in her rows. From each victimized leaf, she plucked off the grubs and popped off their heads. She saved the hornworms in a basket, for bait when fishing at the brook with her boys on some Saturday evening when they were permitted a few daylight hours away from the field, away from the heat, away from Prosser's man.

In the tobacco rows, Gabriel went behind Ma, pinching back the long suckers. Ma reminded him, now and then, to wipe the sticky tar from his bare arms and hands. Solomon came next down the line, topping off the flowers to keep the tobacco from going to seed.

Around noon, the man blew the breakfast horn for the first meal of the day. Some workers knelt and ate their sweet potatoes in the field. Some ran back to the quarter to check on the little children. Gabriel and Solomon fought over who would care for Ma. The tobacco field offered no easy shade, no cooling breeze. While the boys argued, Ma stood and arched her back—low, middling, and high up—then collapsed into the yellow-green leaves. The thick tobacco canopy closed up around her.

Solomon bossed Gabriel, "Run, Gabriel. Run get water for your ma."

Gabriel, who was only nine but strong enough to lift Ma up onto his arm, did not run as his brother said do. "I'm taking Ma to rest, Solomon."

"Rest here!" Solomon shouted. "If the man finds her gone, be hell to pay—a whippin' for you both and likely a whippin' for me, too, Brother."

Gabriel kept walking, with his arm around Ma's waist. He hollered to his older brother, "Don't let him find us! Stir the roosters; make up a fuss. We'll get back before the second horn blows."

So Solomon ran; Solomon made a ruckus that drove Prosser's man toward the house and away from the field while Gabriel tended to Ma.

In the fallow meadow below the tobacco, Gabriel helped his ma to the shade under the low branches of their apple tree. Its king blooms and petals had already fallen, and the crisp, eager smell of new fruit set upon the hillside breeze. Nearby, great whorls of honeysuckle softened the edges between the old field and the ancient forest. All sorts of songbirds darted about the forest glade, flashing gold, cobalt, and, now and again, cherry red. The clover would go uncut until time came to make hay.

Stretching out her swollen feet into the cool clover to comfort them, Ma scraped her thumbnail down each of her fingertips to clear away the green hornworm crust built up from her morning's work. Her dress was wet from sweat, as if she had waded into water to her neck, wearing all her clothes.

Gabriel thought of her going back to the field, bending over the tobacco plants in the full sun. *Let the grubs and suckers ruin all the 'baccy. She's done enough today.*

"Too hot for you to be working so hard, Ma." He tore the tail from his own shirt—his only shirt—and wiped the sweat from her face. In the distance, he heard the faint, low call of the first work horn. People would soon set down their children; the man would soon start his count.

Ma patted her son's leg. "My baby, run on. I'll

come along. Get to the field before that man finds you with me. Run on, now."

"Let him come on. Why am I scared of him?" Gabriel bit his bottom lip to stop its trembling.

Ma smiled at her youngest. "Should have named you Daniel, hmmm? Scared of nothin', run from nothin', walk right on into the lion's den. Daniel." His mother braced against the trunk of the young tree, and in return their tree cradled her body and her burden in its bend.

Ma called on God to keep put the child inside her and let this new one live to play under Gabriel's tree. Ma still believed, now that the war was ended and a new America waking, that freedom would surely soon come.

Gabriel traced the rise and fall of each birthing pain across Ma's face. His eyes fell toward her hands, pulling her knees up high. From someplace dark in Ma, he saw the blood soaking her dress red. Ma cried out, "'My God, I take refuge in you—save me from all my pursuers and rescue me!'"

Because he wanted to please Ma, Gabriel recited the next verse. "'Or my enemy will savage me like a lion, carry me off with no one to rescue me.'"

The second work horn sounded. Ma pressed against the tree and stroked her stomach while the blood continued to flow; Gabriel wiped pearls of sweat from her brow. He blew a cool breath over Ma's temple, the way she always did for him on every August night.

Ma leaned on Gabriel to deliver her fourth son. The child crowned quickly and, with a cord wrapped around his neck, took not one breath.

Holding her stillborn infant close to her heart, Ma said to Gabriel, "Your brother here, he's like Pa. Little One couldn't wait around for freedom to reach Brookfield. He went on made his own way free, your brother."

The house dogs bayed. Gabriel heard shouting in the distance. "Ma?" He shook her shoulder. "Somebody's coming."

Gabriel knew his brother might have confessed. *Solomon looks after Solomon first.*

"What do we say when Mr. Prosser's man comes for us?" he asked Ma.

Ma shut her eyes and continued the psalm. "'God is a shield that protects me, savin' the honest of heart.'"

At Ma's neck and in the tuck of her arms, spilling out of her dress, Gabriel saw the whip marks made not so long ago by Prosser's man. Her wounds were pale scars now, all healed up. Gabriel's hidden wounds, however, cut even deeper. *Let Ma do the praying,* he thought. *One day, I'll fight for our freedom like Pa.*

Gabriel fought no one that day, but he did run up to the great house to fetch Mrs. Prosser. He pleaded for the missus to intervene. Ann Prosser protected them, and neither Gabriel nor Ma nor Solomon got whipped. The next day they buried the little dead child with all of the others who had passed over, and Ma returned to the field. Gabriel went back to his lessons with Thomas Henry Prosser.

CHAPTER FOUR
August 1786

GABRIEL LOVED THOMAS HENRY like a brother. From the beginning, Thomas Henry Prosser had suckled at one side of Ma while Gabriel nursed at the other. When the boys were babies, Gabriel and Ma had even lived in the great house and slept on the nursery floor, so that if the infant master ever cried from hunger, Ma would be right there.

In those days, Ma ate what the family ate. In the kitchen behind the house, Kissey fed Ma fried asparagus, delicate breads, and nourishing meats to keep her strong and full and ready for little Thomas Henry. Bundled up and placed together, the two babies often napped close to the cooking fire.

Once they reached schooling age, Mrs. Prosser began to teach her son reading and writing and mathematics. She taught Gabriel, too, because the young Prosser boy stayed restless and anxious if his milk brother went too far away.

And in turn, Gabriel taught Thomas Henry the songs from the quarter. So Thomas Henry and Old Major, on the fiddle, together would perform for family from Amherst or friends from Richmond. Sometimes, Kissey would sneak Gabriel into the great house and set him crouched in the dark foyer to watch his friend sing the quarter songs in the parlor. He loved to hear the Prossers' blue-silk-and-black-velvet-clad guests praise the quarter songs and would have liked to have stood and sung alongside Thomas Henry.

Gabriel especially loved how Old Major's eyes would find his and share a secret nod that asked, "Can you hear the folks, son? Can you hear them? Shine up; shine out, now." Then, cloaked away in the stairwell, Gabriel would listen and hear in the music all that the velvet-and-silk people could never know—not even his playmate, Thomas Henry. For Old Major could fill the merriest tune with the running of a river or the calling of a road spilling over with kin and leading them all away to someplace green, someplace open, and someplace free.

As Gabriel neared the age that he would be put to work for Brookfield, he and Thomas Henry still entertained themselves with all sorts of games, day and night. When they played hide-and-seek in the great house, if their voices turned too loud or if they got too up under her skirt, Kissey would shoo them out to the yard. There, along Brookfield's poplar-lined drive, the boys pretended to be Virginia patriots — James Monroe or George Washington.

Playing war under the old trees, they argued over who should get the part of Patrick Henry. The boys knew all about the brave Mr. Henry. Many times they had heard Mr. Prosser brag to his friends of how his good friend Mr. Henry had roused a gathering of men upon the church hill in Richmond with a strong and stirring speech.

"I was named for him!" Thomas Henry bragged, as if his father's friendship with the popular orator, now governor of Virginia, should make a difference.

"Well, I was named for the archangel, and it's my turn," Gabriel reasoned.

"My father served in the legislature with Patrick Henry."

"My grandfather was a king!" Gabriel told his friend what Pa had once told him.

Thomas Henry rolled his eyes. "Do you even know what the legislature is, Gabriel?"

"Yes."

"Can you even spell *legislature*?"

Gabriel fidgeted around and looked away, up to the sky. Mrs. Prosser had yet to teach them that word; still, he said, "Of course I can. Can you?"

"Would I have asked you?" Thomas Henry kicked at a dead and downed poplar limb, then bent to wipe the rotten crumbles from his shoe buckle. "Besides, your grandfather was no king. He came to Brookfield from Lancaster County, from Robert King Carter. I read of the purchase in my grandfather's book. King Carter was the only king to come from Lancaster!" The Prosser boy laughed, and Gabriel's face turned red-hot.

Lately, Thomas Henry seemed obsessed with King Carter, and he would not be quiet.

"You're all kin, Gabriel, don't you know that? Westbrook, Half Sink, Spring Meadow, all started with hands bought from King Carter. I'm going to be rich as he was when I'm a man," said Thomas Henry.

Gabriel thought to sock Thomas Henry in the

mouth—a sure guarantee of a lashing—but he heard something different in the boy's crowing this time.

Are all of us here in Henrico descended of the same African king? Could folks from all the quarters for miles and miles be one big, scattered family? Is everybody related to everybody? He needed to get Ma; she could tell him.

"Anyway, your father was only my father's black-smith until he . . ." Thomas Henry stopped when he saw Gabriel turn to leave.

My father came from great men, and, just like Patrick Henry, he fought for the greatest cause, Gabriel reminded himself. He took off for the tobacco field; he knew he would find Ma there.

Thomas Henry followed after him. "Where are you going?" Thomas Henry demanded to know.

"I'd rather pop hornworms," Gabriel muttered. *And imagine one of them is you.*

"You're supposed to stay with me today!" Thomas Henry shouted.

Gabriel kept walking.

When Thomas Henry saw that Gabriel truly meant to leave him, the child's breathing turned shallow and his palms grew sticky. "I'll let you be Patrick Henry!" Thomas Henry shouted.

So Gabriel ran back.

He stood tall in a stream of light shining through the crown of a century oak and onto the chestnut stump. Thomas Henry squatted in the moss, rubbing his chin, playing a statesman. Two squirrels froze halfway down the oak; a nice flock of killdee swooped into the grass.

The old stump felt smooth and warm under Gabriel's bare feet. With a deep bow to his playmate, he closed his eyes and waited for the most famous, most talked-about part of that speech to find its easy voice in his heart. Gabriel thought of Pa, not Patrick Henry. Then he imagined he was his own grandfather, a captive king, speaking to his people.

Gabriel let the birds settle, and then he began. "'Is life so dear, or peace so sweet, as to be purchased at the price of chains and slavery?'" he recited. "'Forbid it, Almighty God!'"

Just behind and beside him, Gabriel noticed that Mr. Prosser now stood, watching them pretend. To show off for the head of Brookfield, when he reached his favorite part, Gabriel folded his right arm across his chest and raised his left to heaven. "'I know not what course others may take, but as for me, give me liberty or give me death!'"

A blue vein flared in Thomas Henry's temple,

and Gabriel knew he had delivered the speech well. Thomas Henry jumped up, shook his fist, and shouted, "'To arms! To arms!'"

The boys grabbed makeshift weapons. Gabriel took up a handful of rocks; Thomas Henry took up a stick. They joined hands to charge the battlefield and stir the killdee. Before the boys could take possession of the imaginary earthworks, Mr. Prosser lurched at Gabriel and shook him by the ear. "Enough! Who thought up to make this mockery?" A vein bulged from Mr. Prosser's temple, too.

Gabriel tucked the rocks and his hands in his pockets and wished he knew the secret way to send his true self deep away into the century oak. No one had yet shown him how.

Thomas Henry spoke first. "It was Gabriel's idea, Father. He always wants to be Patrick Henry and play war."

"Is that true, Gabriel?"

Gabriel kept his tongue still. Over the years, he had learned to let Thomas Henry do the explaining.

Mr. Prosser sent his son away up to the house.

"Do you play this game in the quarter?" Mr. Prosser demanded to know of Gabriel.

Gabriel searched the yard for Kissey to help him.

Of everyone at Brookfield, only Kissey knew what-all could calm Mr. Prosser. Ma said Kissey had practically reared the master herself from the time she was ten and Mr. Prosser but a babe, but Kissey was nowhere to be seen and Mr. Prosser stood waiting for an answer.

Every day Gabriel thought about how Pa had been dragged away for wanting freedom, so he refused to answer even when Mr. Prosser twisted his ear.

"No more war play," Mr. Prosser finally said. "I won't tolerate such poisonous talk. I learned that lesson from your father. Come with me," Mr. Prosser said, and pulled Gabriel along behind him.

When they reached the overseer's dwelling, Prosser's man came out and hooked Gabriel around the neck.

"Knock some sense into the boy," Mr. Prosser ordered.

Gabriel saw his friend's shoes poking out from behind the woodshed. *Thomas Henry's come*, he thought. *I see him there; he's come to help me.* Sure and relieved that he would not be beaten, Gabriel waved for the young master to step out. He smiled in comfort that Thomas Henry was truehearted after all.

Prosser's man smiled, too. With a force Gabriel was unprepared to absorb, the man struck Gabriel's chest and face and back with a wooden board. Had Gabriel expected those first quick blows, he might have stopped the single yelp from escaping. Instead, Gabriel teetered between gasping breath and no breath at all. Bright white blinded one eye, and from the other he saw Brookfield's red ochre dirt and watched the man's brown pants rush toward him.

He dropped to the ground and lay there until both his eyes found, again, the full blue, empty clear sky. Warm rocks tumbled around his mouth. He tried to figure how they had gotten there all the way from his pocket. He spit and turned sick at the sight of his two front teeth swimming in his blood spittle.

Mr. Prosser had just watched. Now the master shouted toward where Thomas Henry hid. "Son, get out from behind the shed. If you're grown enough to defy me, I expect you're man enough to finish this yourself."

Thomas Henry will never hurt me. We go for brothers; everyone says so.

Prosser's man handed the bloodied board to Thomas Henry.

"Don't be chickenhearted, Son. Gabriel must learn his place," said Mr. Prosser. "Are you a man?"

"I am a man, Father," Thomas Henry insisted.

Gabriel covered his face and he rolled onto his side.

The boy struck at Gabriel's head and his legs and his bare feet, then dropped the board and sprinted away.

"Do you understand now?" Mr. Prosser asked Gabriel.

Gabriel nodded that he did.

"Good." Mr. Prosser pulled Gabriel up. "I've always liked you especially well, Gabriel. Go see Kissey for a poultice to stop that bleeding, all right?"

Within earshot of Gabriel, Prosser's man said, "Idle African hands are no good for Brookfield, Mr. Prosser. Negroes that can read and write are dangerous. I expect ones the size of him 'specially so. Considerin' he got his father in him, you might take some action, sir."

"I well know how to control my own bondmen," Mr. Prosser barked. Then he joked, "Controlling my wife is an altogether different matter. I mean to speak to Ann again. She favors Gabriel terribly, indulges him on an almost daily basis. Still, I admire her charitable heart."

The overseer shook his head and pointed at Gabriel. He opened his mouth to speak, but Mr. Prosser interrupted him. "You're right, of course. A boy like Gabriel has a busy mind—too busy." The planter called after Gabriel, "Tell your mother I'm sending you to Richmond."

"Yes, sir," Gabriel said, and he ran to the quarter for Ma and Kissey.

The words *I'm sending you to Richmond* might have caused some other boy to take to the marsh, but Gabriel was descended from a family long in greatness and courage. Richmond petrified Ma, but a mere city could not frighten Gabriel.

CHAPTER FIVE
September 1786

MA KNEW that Mr. Prosser determined the life's work of Brookfield's people. She had no voice for herself and no voice for her sons. When Gabriel had come to her saying, "I'm going to Richmond," she could only let him go.

Even though Pa had been taken away, tradition declared that Pa's trade would rightfully pass to his sons. Solomon, who had just turned eleven, would learn to smith, and Mr. Prosser had arranged that Gabriel would join his brother as an apprentice. The two younger sons of Brookfield's former blacksmith would learn their new trade together, and they would learn in the city.

Ma thought Gabriel might make as fine a smithy as Pa and, she reckoned, an even better one than Solomon, but still she prayed, *Not yet, Lord.* She could do nothing more than pray; Mr. Prosser had decided.

What can a woman do, Lord?

On the night before her sons were to leave, the pine knots in the fire had nearly all burned up, and Ma watched Gabriel twitching restlessly on the floor. She placed her hand on his chest to calm his fitfulness.

"Gabriel." She tried to soothe him into a peaceful sleep. "Settle down, now. Sleep if you can. Settle down."

If Mr. Prosser's plot to send Gabriel to Richmond didn't scare Gabriel, it did Ma. She had seen that city tear apart many families, including her own.

Why come Gabriel's goin' there now, when I still need him here, only the Lord knows, she thought. *No good thing come from bein' in Richmond.*

Ma had once been one of the women standing exposed in the bottom of that town. She had stood on the wood wearing only a modest soiled muslin cloth knotted around her waist.

Every day still, some buried but not forgotten hurt swelled through her. Now'days Ma never knew whether the bad memory might be roused by the sweet-earth smell of Richmond's bad tobacco burning on the wind or awakened by Prosser's man pausing to bend and stare her down. She never knew what might drive the terrible recollections back into the forefront of her brain; she only knew the evil imposed on her could not be suppressed inside her. Every day, still, in muscle and mind and skin, she remembered how the trader had, for the bidding crowd, held up first her left breast and then her right, as if testing fruit for its prime. Even folding over tobacco plants or handling holiday turkeys with Kissey might suck Ma right back to that day.

She was only a girl and her bleeding had only just started. At first, she had not understood when the trader called her a good breeder, but when he then invited Mr. Prosser and the other bidding men to remove the muslin in order to squeeze her hips and examine the between of her thighs, she understood. Standing there outside the courthouse facing the James River in Richmond, she had prayed the river might sweep her away home. Once she realized she could never go back, she prayed she might never bleed again.

Now, after so many years of holding herself prisoner to her past, Ma tried to set free her mind from the terrible thoughts and memories of that day, let them all fly away with smoke from the dwindling fire.

Virginia Gazette, JULY 10, 1762

ADVERTISEMENT

*J*ust arrived in James *River,* from Old
Callabar, The *Anne* Galley, Capt. *Alexander
Robe,* with a Cargoe of choice healthy Slaves,
the Sale of which will begin at *Richmond town,*
on *Friday,* the 16th, of this Instant month and
there be continued 'til all are sold.

She knelt down beside Gabriel and blew her cool breath across his face. *If I gave a good increase for Mr. Prosser, it's only 'cause I love the blacksmith so.*

To lure away all the suffering that her tired mind liked to unleash in these kinds of still moments, Ma hummed out loud. To fill herself up with today, right now, only this instant of watching her boy sleep, Ma stroked Gabriel's brow. Yet somehow, the stubborn taproot of the worst yesterday of all refused to loosen its hold, and she remembered.

She remembered how Prosser's man had come to the quarter to fetch Pa in the darkest strand of earliest morning. Pa's trade had often sent him away from Brookfield around the countryside or into the city, and Ma could always sense his returns. The last time Pa left, Ma knew he would not be back.

Pa hadn't time to explain or run before the overseer showed up with a gun. When she saw that Prosser's man was armed, Ma had figured the truth. *Pa been talkin' again—here, there, all over—about us risin', about us bein' free. Mr. Prosser had enough now.*

"I'm goin' to Richmond," Pa had told his family.

Ma could only nod. "Couldn't make a better man than you, the Lord. You find a way back to me, Pa.

Hear me? No better man." Her hands had started to shake in fear and in rage. Ma considered whether she had the strength to seize the gun from Prosser's man and strike him down.

If I kill the man now with my bare hands, will this be over or will it just be startin'? Could we make our way?

On the still-dark morning that Prosser's man took Pa to Richmond, Gabriel had grabbed a hold of his father's pant leg. That act had quelled Ma's murderous thinking.

"I want to come with you, Pa," Gabriel had begged, and Ma peeled her boy from his father. She saw then that she needed to be Gabriel's mother more than she needed to slay a man.

Her husband had always told her, "I see the place in you that no man can ever harm. Not Prosser. Not his man. I belong there." Pa knew that place. Pa. No one else.

Then Ma fell to her knees, too, and wrapped her own self around Pa. "I can't stay without you; I don't want to. You find your way back to me," she said, again.

"I will, Ma. I will." Pa had tried to lift her up, but Ma spread full out on the floor.

"I'm goin' to Richmond now. I'll be all right," her

husband had said. Pa kissed Martin and Solomon, and Ma. He put his lips to Gabriel's ear. "Be brave, and you will be free, my angel-boy."

While revisiting the memory of that horrid day, Ma had let the fire completely die out in their hut. Not a curl of smoke lingered; nothing to carry this memory away, so Ma stopped tugging on the taproot. She knew this one would only grow stronger.

What can a poor woman do, Lord?

She lifted her sleeping youngest son to the bed and took his place on the floor.

In the morning, she stood beside Prosser's cart and watched Old Major and the bay mare take two of her sons away. She jogged along next to the cart, holding Gabriel's hand through the bars.

Ma didn't worry as much about Solomon. *Solomon follows, but Gabriel, he leads by his own mind. Trouble creeps along after a strong and willful boy like him. Pa would be proud. Lord, I am scared.*

"Solomon, take care of Gabriel. Keep your brother safe," she pleaded.

Ma ran faster to keep up and would not let go of Gabriel's hand. "I don't like Richmond," she cried. "Come back to me." Mr. Prosser urged Old Major to whip the bay mare away faster.

"I will, Ma. I will," Gabriel called out to her, and then let go of Ma's hand.

She prayed again. *Set your light upon Solomon and Gabriel, Lord, bring my boys home. Bring them home from Richmond and back to me one day.*

CHAPTER SIX
September 1786

GABRIEL DREW IN a deep breath through the space of his missing front teeth. *Richmond,* he thought. *Solomon and me must be mighty important, going to Richmond.*

Since his birth at Brookfield, Gabriel had left the plantation only for worship or, sometimes, for a fish feast. Not once had Gabriel strayed from the country-side, and when he did travel to Young's spring or Brook Bridge, he kept to the forest. Early on, Pa had taught him to avoid the roads because even those who held remit passes could still fall prey to the watch patrol. Even when he carried a permit, Gabriel was accustomed to hearing Ma or Pa or Martin shout, "Get to the woods!"

No matter how thick the trees or dense the brush, he wasn't scared of the forest, and he told himself he wouldn't be scared of Richmond, either. Still, in the cart Gabriel sat so close to his brother—so close— that Solomon hung an arm and a leg through the bars to find himself more room.

Both boys fidgeted to get more comfortable; Mrs. Prosser had dressed them each in Thomas Henry's discarded clothing—itchy brown vests and knickers and well-worn buckle shoes that pinched their feet.

Pressed up against his brother, Gabriel watched Brookfield disappear from sight. The two-story white manor house with eleven front windows and east and west wings—each with its own brick chimney—was the finest man-made place known to Gabriel.

What will we see in the capital? he wondered. *How long before we get there?*

The way was worn into a road packed hard over time by travelers from the countryside and around the state, going to the city to trade or visit. The bay mare could have gotten the boys to Richmond on her memory alone, for she and Old Major traveled there regularly on business for Mr. Prosser. In just over an hour, the cart had traveled six miles along the winding, wooded trace from Brookfield into the

Prosser's Brookfield

capital. Occasional sweet blasts of honeysuckle—Ma's favorite—perfumed the roadside. Each time Gabriel caught a whiff, his confidence in his surroundings grew.

Finally, Solomon pointed south to a low black cloud forming a long black line, just above the treetops. "There's your Richmond," Solomon said.

Gabriel's eyes grew wide. "Is the city on fire?" He drew even closer to his brother, who pushed him off and said, "Coal, stupid."

A coal cloud made of ash from chimneys and smithies and river mills draped the capital. The Richmond road was nothing but bare, fresh-cut earth; no rocks or brick led travelers from the woods into the unfinished city.

Richmond had been the capital for only six years, since Virginia moved it there from Williamsburg to keep its seat safe from the British during the war. Hands from all over the countryside now came to help build houses and cut new roads. Mr. Prosser had even hired out Gabriel's brother Martin to work on the capitol building, for, like the city itself, the statehouse stood partly unfinished.

Gabriel thought Thomas Jefferson's capitol, high atop Shockoe Hill, was much finer than Brookfield. All the land had been cleared around the white, rectangular building, with Roman columns that lined a sweeping portico looking out over the river.

My brother helped make this place, and now Solomon and me will build the city, too.

Gabriel stared at black men hammering the capitol roof alongside white and pointed out how others, together, rolled hogsheads of tobacco down the narrow Richmond roads. Soldiers of the public guard lazed about on the grounds, playing cards and slapping backs. Pigs and sheep wandered with no apparent purpose, content to follow along after whoever held the next probable meal, until some knowing hand prodded them back to their lowly places.

As Mr. Prosser's gig rounded the bend and turned down past the capitol, a strong rain came up. Without a green grassy field or a fine floral garden to hold the earth in place, the dirt piles and loose rocks bordering the capitol square right away began to slide into the narrow road. Two long ditches had eroded along each side of the nearly done statehouse, and now rainwater rushed to fill them.

The shower had come up so fast that it caught the chattel and workers alike off their guard. The cows and sheep, pigs and chickens, that roamed the barren grounds scrambled over and up the ditches. They gathered on the capitol's portico and huddled around its columns, depositing a muddy tangle of hoof- and footprints. Gabriel laughed out loud and wondered what the governor would think of the barnyard on the statehouse porch. Soldiers spilled from their barracks—parading across the capitol grounds in their long underwear—to snatch up the uniforms they had left spread out to dry on the hard clay that was now turning to muck.

Gabriel welcomed the rain; he turned his face up. *Maybe all this water will stretch out these shoes*, he thought, and he stamped his feet in the puddle collecting on the gig's floor.

Two shackled oxen walked along so close behind them that Gabriel could feel the steam rolling out their nostrils on his legs. One of them grunted when Mr. Prosser's mare stopped in the street to do her business. The men driving the oxen yelled, "Move it!" Then Old Major popped the mare to make her walk on.

Around the bend from the capitol, a black tavern-keep chucked a white man right out into the road. The hairy drunkard landed in a hole with a great splash that soiled Gabriel's shirt, but Gabriel didn't care. He watched the drunk man tuck into his knees and cover his head with his hands in fear of getting trampled by the beasts in the road.

It seemed to Gabriel that everyone in Richmond wanted to be in the road. And the road wanted to get to the river.

Even up on Shockoe Hill, Gabriel could hear the James River roaring below them. He stood up in the cart, expecting to see great, high falls. But the falls of the James made a shallow, descending staircase of rocks, rapids, and ripples that caused its waters to swirl and spray around two forest islands. Tobacco warehouses and flour mills clustered around the falls to harness the river's power and send the city's goods downriver and out to sea, out to the world.

As if they didn't even mind the rain, some washerwomen squatted near Shockoe Creek with their baskets of laundry, quarreling with one another over who should do what to collect the now-drenched clothes and bedsheets that had been earlier laid out to dry across the grassy meadow below the market house. Gabriel saw no overseer to keep the peace or keep them quiet; the washerwomen went about their work, and they went about their fussing, too.

Gabriel breathed in deep. He smelled the familiar burn of sweet, rich leaves. "Tobacco?" he guessed.

Solomon scoffed. "Can't you figure anything out for yourself?"

Gabriel elbowed his brother and scooted all the way to the other end of the bench. He saw how everyone and everything in Richmond had someplace to be. *Is everyone here free to work and walk where they please?* Gabriel wondered.

The youngest laundress, a girl no older than Gabriel, tried to shoo an old dog away before four dirty, wet paws could discover how freshly washed shirts make a fine, easy treasure to snatch. Drenched and matted, the dog cocked an ear and appeared to laugh at the washerwomen as it pounced and dragged a white sheet through a shallow freshet off the creek.

"Rascal!" cried the young laundress, but the mongrel had vanished with its prize to someplace hidden, dark, and safe in Richmond. The mutt should have made Gabriel homesick for Dog, or even Kissey, or Ma.

Instead, Gabriel thought of Pa.

And because he did not know for certain where Pa was gone away to, only that he had last been sent to Richmond, Gabriel could not stop himself, when the gig passed by the mills, from looking for his pa in the faces of the big men unloading grain sacks.

At the bottom of the hill, the powerful roar of the river excited Gabriel. He let himself imagine whether, if he kept still in the current, the bubbling white water might carry him all the way to his father, wherever that might be.

Along Main Street, Old Major sped up the cart to outrun the rain. The city people crowded together to cross the stone footbridge over Shockoe Creek. The mare forded the creek at the trot and doused the people good; the women squealed and the men cursed. Gabriel fell off his seat onto the floor.

"Get up!" Solomon barked, but held his hand out to help his brother. "Now, act right or they'll throw you in there." Solomon pointed to an open-air jail near the market house. A tangle of arms and faces reached through its bars. Prisoners waved their limbs in the rain, straining to wash clean what they could of their rank skin.

"What is that?" Gabriel asked.

"The Cage, of course. It's where they keep people who can't stay out of trouble. Pa told me so; he told me all about Richmond."

No man in the Cage had even a square foot of space to himself. Some of the prisoners feigned sleep;

others urinated between the bars and into the road. Gabriel tried not to look for Pa in there. He didn't want any of those faces to be Pa's.

Solomon scooted over close to Gabriel. "Look." He pointed. "See those eyes watching you? Runaways. Troublemakers. Thieves." Solomon whispered in Gabriel's ear, "Careful in the city, Little Brother."

Gabriel made himself turn away. "Ma said you're supposed to take care of me," he said, and he kicked Solomon in the shin.

Before Solomon could kick him back, the cart stopped in front of a wooden shack along the north bank of the river, below the white water and beyond the courthouse.

Old Major unlatched the cart's door. Mr. Prosser said, "Out you get! Hurry up. This will be your home for the next seven years, boys."

The day's adventure had distracted Gabriel, but now he looked to Old Major for help that did not come. Solomon began to cry, so Gabriel drew up the courage to utter two words: "Seven years?"

"What did you think? That we were making a day trip?" Mr. Prosser answered.

"No. I—thought—" Gabriel realized that he had

thought only of traveling to the capital. "When will we see Ma again?"

Mr. Prosser grunted; his temper flared across his face. Mr. Prosser raised his hand to strike, and Gabriel drew back.

Get to the woods! He thought he heard Ma whisper, but the best trees in the city were at the top of the hill or on the river islands. In the bottom of Richmond, he saw no woods thick enough to hide a boy but for a few minutes and not a single tree stand dense enough to ward patrollers away.

Even if I knew where to run, Gabriel thought, *I'd have to get these shoes off first.*

There would be no getting anyplace for now, but Gabriel had already made a city map in his mind.

It's still not so different here, he thought. *No paths through the forest, but alleyways aplenty. A creek for bathing and a riverbank for gathering. No great house always in sight, but the white shadow of the statehouse sitting high on the hill. And not one person's been stopped, because they all have business here. Now I have my business, too.*

CHAPTER SEVEN
September 1786

GABRIEL STUCK CLOSE BEHIND Mr. Prosser, and Solomon behind Gabriel. Without knocking, and as if the place belonged to him, Mr. Prosser entered the small wood house.

The Henrico planter hollered into the empty front room, "Thomas Prosser here!" Then Mr. Prosser banged on the open front door with his fist and called out to the blacksmith, "Jacob Kent?"

A hearty man of powerful build, wearing a gray shirt that Gabriel figured used to be white, greeted them. The blacksmith also wore a leather apron around his waist; its pockets bulged out and flowed over with tools and nails and debris. From one, he pulled out a soiled cloth and dabbed his flushed, wet face.

Gabriel whispered to his brother, "That's the pinkest man I ever saw."

Solomon laughed and elbowed Gabriel's ribs. "Shhh. He keeps the bones of boys gone bad in that apron of his."

Gabriel noticed that the smith's boots were black and cracked, just like Pa's. Jacob Kent's feet made even Mr. Prosser's thin ones look like a lady's. *Why, his head would touch the ceiling if he didn't crouch down.* Gabriel realized he was staring, but he could think only of how the master smith reminded him of Pa.

"Welcome, sir," Jacob Kent said to Mr. Prosser. "Are these my new smiths-in-waiting?" The blacksmith placed a callused hand on Gabriel's shoulder.

Like Pa used to do. Gabriel sighed. *I should be learning from Pa, not some old, pink smithy.*

Once Mr. Prosser left, Gabriel felt brave enough to copy the gesture he had seen Thomas Henry use with Mr. Prosser's friends, and he offered his hand to the blacksmith. "Hello. I'm Gabriel, sir, and this is my brother Solomon."

Jacob shook Gabriel's hand and met his eye. "Gabriel Prosser, good to know you." The blacksmith nodded.

Gabriel looked about, and, still seeing no woods

to get to but feeling ever more confident to speak, he said, "No, sir, not Prosser. I'm just Gabriel."

"Well, just-Gabriel, welcome!" The blacksmith laughed, and Gabriel saw that Jacob Kent had also lost his own front teeth.

"Your younger brother, then?" Jacob motioned to Solomon, who shook his head no but managed to say only, "Older."

"Just-Gabriel and Older-Solomon. All right, I'm straight now: the bigger one is the young 'un."

Gabriel liked that Jacob Kent wore no wig but tied up his long black hair with a long black ribbon. Set against an unshaven chin and deep cracks in his face, Jacob's pale-blue eyes surprised Gabriel. *Maybe he's different*, Gabriel thought, but then he remembered Pa's warning. *There is no such thing as a good and kind master.*

"Are you our new master?" Gabriel asked the smithy. He didn't let Jacob Kent answer. "Have we been sold away from Brookfield? Will we see our ma again?"

Jacob placed an arm around the shoulder of each brother and drew them nigh. "Hardly my own master, so no, not yours. I'll be your teacher, just as I taught your father. Now, let me show you around my place. You two can show me how well you can hammer."

The smith stopped in the breezeway between the house and forge and stared down at the boys' feet. "Need to find you each a pair of boots like mine." He laughed. "You'll outgrow 'em in no time." Jacob handed Gabriel a leather apron of his own, and Solomon one, too. "You'll see your mother again. I promise."

I could like a good and kind teacher very much, Gabriel told himself. *Especially if Jacob Kent taught Pa.* That thought sparked the desire in Gabriel to learn all that he could. He would miss Ma and Dog and Kissey and Old Major, but mostly Gabriel intended to work too hard to pay attention to the lonely twinges of his heart. He also promised himself that he would learn the river city as well as he knew the forest countryside.

CHAPTER EIGHT
November 1786

FROM JACOB'S FORGE, Gabriel could hear the constant, distant roar of the James River falls, and he could see the reaches of the sycamore on the north bank near the river's bend west. The autumn oasis of golden leaves and marbled bark collided with a white canvas of muslin sails from the ships that crowded Richmond's port, bringing in goods or taking away riches. He missed swimming off the river islands on Sundays, as he had all throughout the early autumn, but the cold November river meant one thing less to distract him from the forge.

Jacob Kent demanded his place be kept orderly and clean. It was Gabriel's job to straighten the smithy at night and ready the work in the morning. He liked rising in the dark, arranging the charcoal in the heart of the forge, waking the great bellows, and making ready the fire.

The washerwomen also made their wash fires, over by Shockoe Creek, before the sun made day. Each morning, rain or shine, August heat or November cold, Gabriel would visit the creek to collect water to fill the horse trough outside the smithy door. The youngest laundress, a girl named Nanny, who had been sold away from her family in the mountains, taught him where to find the coolest part of the creek. Every day, Gabriel and Nanny spoke of fire and water and nothing more.

When his morning chores were complete—the fire built, the floor cleaned, and the anvils ready for the coming day—he would walk back to the Shockoe and there fill three ceramic jugs with drinking water. Once the water jugs were set within easy reach of each anvil so that Jacob, Solomon, and he could refresh themselves throughout the long day, Gabriel would wake Jacob and Solomon with three full strikes to his anvil.

Ping, ping, ping. Gabriel signaled when the fire was hot and the forge ready. *Ping, ping, ping.* He wondered if the whole of Richmond waited to hear his anvil beat, for his wake-up bell would often bring in a horse or two to be shod, a rifle or a pistol for repair, or an urgent plea to fix a broken-off key. Nearly all the workings of the capital city could be made or repaired with a fire, an anvil, and a hammer or two.

At the start of each day and in between jobs, Gabriel and Solomon forged nails. So many new houses and public buildings and shops were going up that Richmond could use every nail the boys would make and more. Between them, the two brothers produced eight thousand nails a week. Fifty thousand would not have satiated the capital city.

When Jacob was pleased with their work, he let the boys know. "Very nice. Coming along," he would commend Solomon.

Once, when Jacob examined a long nail forged by Gabriel, the teacher purposefully pricked his finger on the tip. "You're scaring me, son," he said, and sucked the blood the nail drew. Jacob pushed his eyeglasses higher onto his face with the back of his wrist and shook his head at the work Gabriel presented.

"Beg pardon, sir?" Gabriel said. He thought his own work finer than his brother's, yet the teacher had complimented only Solomon.

"Show me how you did this." Jacob shot up his

wild, curly eyebrows and nodded for Gabriel to forge another.

Gabriel set the plain rolled iron in the fire. He pulled the bellows—what Jacob called the lung of the smithy—so that it would blow a deep breath over the coals.

"Back off a bit, son. That's good. Coax the fire—don't force it," said Jacob.

Gabriel turned the iron bar now and again until it glowed a devilish white. He rested the iron at a sharp angle against the face of the anvil, making sure to keep his hand firm so that no light, air, or heat could escape. Then Gabriel hammered the end, drawing the iron out long and thin. When the plain bar felt the weight of a nail to him, he used a small wedge to mark the cut and hammered until the thin piece fell away; then he set about turning the iron sliver into a sharp nail.

Clang, clang, clang. Ping. Clang, clang, clang. Ping. Gabriel hammered out the tip with an even, steady pace, never missing his mark except on every fourth strike, to settle the hammer in his left palm. Even when Gabriel's hands started to cramp from gripping the hammer and the iron, he kept on heating, turning, hammering, and setting the shape with water.

Soon, four edges emerged. With great patience, he

drew out an even square. When the square met with his satisfaction, Gabriel pressed one edge hard against the anvil. With perfect pacing, his hammer drew forth a perfect tine tip. Then he slipped the nail through the pritchel hole at the anvil's heel, upsetting the iron into an almost-square nail head. After giving it a final dip in the water, Gabriel presented the nail to Jacob.

The master blacksmith shook his head. "Know smiths who've worked for years—smiths been on their own for a good long while—who still can't hammer so well." Jacob took the nail from Gabriel, heated it, and smoothed the metal clean. This was how Gabriel learned—by doing what needed doing and presenting the work to Jacob.

When a farmer from Varina, east of the city, brought in scrap metal to sell or trade—for Jacob Kent believed everything could be reused—Gabriel stood near the teacher to learn all he could about the properties of old steel or iron. When the governor's aide brought His Excellency's steed for shoeing, Gabriel knew to stack the old shoes in the great pile for melting and repurposing later.

What he loved most about the forge, though, was that Jacob and his customers were patriots. Even more than Gabriel enjoyed swimming or fishing in the James

River, he craved the bold talk of the men who filled the dark smithy. While visitors to the forge brought with them new problems to solve, they also often brought new thoughts on the building of America or the spreading of freedom.

All sorts of men gathered there. Artisans, black and white, free and slave, used the forge as a sort of trading place. When coopers and carpenters stopped in to have their tools sharpened or repaired, they borrowed and bartered in the smithy yard while they waited. Bonded hammermen spent short residencies in the forge, too, whenever Jacob needed help with big jobs—such as anchors or chains for ships in port. Free black men searching for work by the river counted on Jacob for odd jobs. All of these men and their business at the forge kept Pa's spirit present and constant before Gabriel.

Gabriel and Solomon grew into fine blacksmiths, and each brother made what he could from the trade. Smithing soothed Solomon's worried mind into a still and easeful peace. Hammering set Gabriel's active mind afire.

CHAPTER NINE
August 1792

GABRIEL WORKED HIS ANVIL in the spot nearest the door so that he could see and hear everything. Richmond was growing from a small town into a global port, and all the while, the wildfire of liberty jumped across the oceans from nation to nation. Patrons with jobs for the smithy or simply with mouths to run and hours to fill rendezvoused daily at the forge to debate and argue and persuade. Local artisans spoke longingly of the ongoing political upheaval in France, while country planters and city merchants whispered fearfully of the revolution on Saint Domingue. In Virginia, the planters and merchants had led the revolution. But on the small Caribbean island, it had been slaves who rose up to declare their freedom, crying, "Death or liberty!" A bloodbath, the merchants called it.

At night, Gabriel and Solomon talked about the world and their work. They lay side by side beneath the window in the small room off the forge where they shared a bed. They had long ago stopped arguing over whether to leave their window shut at night, and with the sash wide open, they heard the usual Friday-night joking and singing from the street. Even the washer-women were out there, crowded onto a single stoop beneath the flickering light of a street lantern, hooting and hollering this evening instead of quarreling. He heard the laundress Nanny out there with them.

Solomon lay on his back, looking at the ceiling. "When I hammer," he told his brother, "I think 'bout each strike; that's all. I watch the fire and, for once, don't worry 'bout you findin' trouble or Ma takin' ill. When I hammer, I even forget they took Pa."

Gabriel fidgeted in the bed; he wanted to be out dancing with the people by the river. He thought how the spray from the broad, rocky falls of the James would keep him cool. He figured a mug of grog, or maybe two, would loosen his fear of Nanny. Maybe tonight he would start a conversation with her, talk about something more than making fire or drawing water. He often noticed how the skinny, long-legged laundress watched him while she pretended not to. Just the other day, she fell right into Shockoe Creek when Gabriel and Solomon walked past. The older women around her had laughed at the girl when it happened. Now Gabriel could hear all of them out there in the street, and he longed to hear Nanny's laughter. He dared not hope to hear her say, "Wish Gabriel would come on and join us tonight."

Solomon interrupted Gabriel's yearning. "What is the forge like for you, Brother?" Solomon asked.

With enough heat, I can turn iron into whatever I please, Gabriel thought. "Fire changes everything," he said. The moon bathed his brother's face, and Gabriel saw Solomon's confusion. He went on. "Hammering helps my mind make sense. If I face a problem, I go to the anvil. I hear and see so much in the city. When I bend over the anvil with my hammer, our people, our worries, and our river all melt together, and all my questions come out like a plan. Do you understand?"

He kicked off the bedsheet. The sounds of the girls and the banjo and the drunkards of August poured through the window and quenched his skin. The sounds of the James tumbling over the bedrock eased his spirit.

The James sets its own course.

He wanted Solomon to understand how his heart was growing and changing from working in the forge, from living in the city. "The tavernkeep next door — the one who sneaks us grog out back — told me a constable arrested the free woman Mrs. Barnett for harboring runaways," he said.

Solomon yawned and scratched his crotch. "That's news to you? Even the free aren't free, Little Brother." Solomon stretched out his legs and took up even more of Gabriel's space in the bed. "Everyone knows Angela Barnett will hang at the gallows. She killed the constable who broke into her house!"

Gabriel sat up. "No, what I'm telling you is, she will live! The laundresses whisper how Mrs. Barnett turned up with child at the jail. I overheard that Nanny tell how all the Richmond ladies have taken up that free woman's cause."

"Your hammer's got good ears, but why bother thinkin' 'bout that? The well-born ladies would never take up for Gabriel or Solomon. The sight of us, just the whiff of our business, offends the well-born ladies. The stench of you is likely what made your laundress, Nanny, end up falling in the creek."

Gabriel started to push Solomon out of the bed,

but suddenly he caught among the sounds outside his window the determined voice of his laundress, sticking up for herself, fending off an unwanted advance. "You might be a free man, but you best keep your free hands to yourself. Only I decide who touches me. I decide," he heard her say.

The crowd of people came to her defense, and he soon heard a boatman apologize. Gabriel smiled to himself. *Uh-uh. No trifling girl for me. Even the laundress knows in her heart what it means to be free. The next time I see Nanny,* he vowed to himself, *I won't shy from talking.*

Fiddling and drumming and voices from the riverbank filled the brothers' tiny room. The moon had made its way westward and left the room dark. Gabriel let the street song flood over him then. While he dreamed, from the city's every corner, every hill, and every hill bottom, a single petition arose in Gabriel's soul: *All over the world, men are taking up the cause of freedom. Who will take up our cause?*

The next morning, Gabriel trotted down to Shockoe Creek to fetch water. As he did every day, he looked for Nanny, but she had vanished. He asked after her of the older women.

"Nan gone to Wilkinson's farm in Henrico," they

told him. "The old colonel's her master. He bought her when she was just a little thing, bought her and took her away from her three sisters in Bedford. She never even met Wilkinson till this morning when he put her in the cart."

"How could that be? She lives here in the city with us. Since the day I got here, Nanny's been here, too." Gabriel rubbed his brow.

"Child, you still a baby inside that grown man's body? Nanny been hired out here in town for all these years. If the colonel says he needs her in the country more than he needs the money he gets for hiring out her sewing and washing, then so it is. A man like you could put some money in his pocket hiring out. You know about hiring out, don't you? But women like us? We just go where we're told. Today, your Nanny was taken away to the country."

Like that, the laundress was gone from the city.

Her Friday-night words rang and rang inside him. *I decide.* She had said it with such conviction that Gabriel had believed her. *I decide.* The offending boatman had believed, too, and all the riverside people. The new day mocked all of them.

CHAPTER TEN
June 1793

GABRIEL LEFT Jacob's forge when he was almost seventeen, returning to Henrico a trained blacksmith, ready to take Pa's place. Throughout his years of absence, he had visited Brookfield during Christmas and, most years, once or twice more.

An unfamiliar distance had grown between Gabriel and Ma, though, either from living in different worlds or from his having grown up without her.

"You're a man now, Gabriel," Ma had said when Gabriel returned. "Nothin' left for me to do but pray the Lord'll keep you safe and grant you some way better than He did for me and Pa. But I'm too tired for much prayin'."

Gabriel saw from the vacancy in Ma's eyes and the heaviness of her step that the years in the field and nights alone had emptied her out. To revive Ma's heart, he told her about life in the city, living and working among all sorts of people, and he told her all he knew about the fight for freedom on Saint Domingue. "Slaves rising up on their own, Ma," he said. "Pa was right. We could, too."

Ma turned away from his talk, but Gabriel persisted. "Slaves, Ma! Doing what Pa dreamed of— winning freedom," he told her. But Ma no longer spoke of Pa or freedom or even much of God. He wondered if she still believed. He did not know for sure if he believed, or exactly what he might believe in. Then he saw his laundress at Young's spring.

The people from Young's and Prosser's and old Colonel Wilkinson's had gathered at the spring, as they were permitted to do on Saturday afternoons and Sundays. The young men fished from the bridge while the young women washed clothes or sat sprawled across the bedrock, talking. Gabriel knew all but one of the girls from the countryside.

When he first saw Nanny again, she wasn't laughing or flirting or drawing attention to herself with the foolish antics displayed by Venus and the other girls. She was sitting beneath a great live oak, plaiting her friend's hair, while Isaac, Jupiter, and Solomon pretended to fight, pulling each other down into the creek. All of Gabriel's friends were clamoring for Nanny's attention, and he couldn't fault them.

He tried to will Nanny to look up at him, but Venus noticed him staring down from the bridge. "Well, well. I see Mister Gabriel up there, spying on us." Venus goaded Gabriel by calling him *mister.* "Why're you comin' down here to the creek? I thought you better than all us now."

Gabriel waved at Nanny; she nodded and glanced away.

Still vying for his attention, Venus teased him again. "The young master been askin' after you, Gabriel. You better get up to the house before too long, now."

Since the day Thomas Henry had beaten Gabriel, then run away, Gabriel had avoided his milk brother. On all his trips back to Brookfield, he had stayed in the quarter or kept to the woods. Never once did Gabriel ask for Thomas Henry or go looking for him. He was not about to go now just because Venus said to, so instead he hollered down to her, "I'll be up sometime to see your ma. We got our birthday coming up.

I made her a new ladle; seems Dog run off with her good one." Then he added, for everyone to hear, "I'm done with Thomas Henry Prosser. I'm done calling any man my master."

When he said that, his friends stopped horsing around and looked about nervously to be sure that neither Prosser's man nor Young's was near. But Nanny looked up and smiled.

"Hush yourself, Gabriel," Venus warned. "Or you'll follow in your pa's footsteps, for sure. I don't need to know how to read to tell that truth."

Emboldened by finding Nanny again, and certain, just from the way she looked at him, that she knew his heart, Gabriel took yet another risk. "Anybody told you about the French island, Venus? All those slaves are free now — they know what my pa knew, and what I know, too."

Venus would not quit. "Oh, you have a master, all right. You're not foolin' nobody."

Nanny defended him. "Venus, what Gabriel means is, a man can never own another man. His spirit soars free as every bird you see," she said.

She knows me, he thought. He tried to move toward her; he tried to speak to her, as he had told himself he would the very next time he saw her. But here in the now of this moment, his wobbly legs and rusty tongue disobeyed his heart.

Gabriel's best friend, Jupiter, set down his fishing pole and tried to talk the girls into a game of chicken-in-the-spring. He pleaded for them to swim with him and Isaac.

"Maybe later," Nanny said without looking away from Gabriel.

Jupiter and Isaac started splashing Nanny. "Come on in here, now, and cool off some," Jupiter said.

Venus urged Nanny to be done already with her hair. "Come on, Nan. Let's go in the water with the boys."

From the bridge, Gabriel watched the foursome, and when, at last, Nanny did stand up and walk to the spring, Gabriel wanted to go with her. He knew Jupiter would have stepped aside and given him this chance with Nanny, but Gabriel had returned to feeling shy. So instead, he stood and watched Jupiter's strong shoulders carry Nanny, and Jupiter's hands grip Nanny's thighs as she pulled Venus and Isaac down into the spring.

Gabriel left his friends and Nanny standing in the creek and ran up to find his ma—to tell her about this girl.

"You sure this girl's not a made-up girl? You sure?" Ma kidded.

He was relieved when Ma teased him.

"The heat from the forge gettin' to you? Makin' you see pretty visions?"

Gabriel didn't try to explain to Ma how the forge gave him not visions but solutions to problems that he faced with the metal, with his friends, with the world.

He knew that before he could truly court Nanny, he would need to settle up with Jupiter, and so he took that problem to the forge and the fire. Now he was a man, a blacksmith, like Pa, and worked in Brookfield's forge, Pa's old forge, his now, too. He drew and upset and punched and cut every sort of iron while he turned his dilemma over in his mind, over in the heat. While he fixed the scythes meant for cutting wheat, he welded the facts and his feelings into one simple act: *Tell Jupiter of my heart for Nanny and keep our friendship true.*

When they next met up in the woods, Gabriel confessed to Jupiter, "You're my friend and we go for brothers, but I think I love Nanny."

"I know," said Jupiter. "It's all right. I might could love her, one day, but I don't yet."

The two friends walked in silence together along

the footpath in the forest that connected Brookfield to Colonel Wilkinson's place. The narrow path forced them to walk in a line; Gabriel led the way.

"What if she doesn't love me back?" Gabriel said after a while.

Jupiter stopped. He draped his arms around Gabriel. "Nanny will love you; you're Gabriel. We all love you, my brother."

Once Gabriel had made his peace with Jupiter, he started his courtship of Nanny. Every Saturday afternoon, after he closed up Prosser's blacksmith shop, Gabriel went down to Young's spring, hoping to see her. He took his fishing pole or he carried Ma's wash. Some days, he walked there with his friends, but he went only to find the girl who could look into his smile and see the deep and secret life inside him. He went to the creek for Nanny to make him right.

CHAPTER ELEVEN
July 1793

GABRIEL ASKED after Nanny each Saturday that arrived without her at the spring. To the women from Wilkinson's—the older ones especially—he'd say, "Nanny coming down tonight? How's Nanny been this week? Expect I'll see my Nanny soon?"

Each Saturday the women answered the same: Nanny had too much work under orders of Wilkinson's man, or her work was done but because he could, the man kept her back. Each passing Saturday, Gabriel sent the women back to Nanny with a gift from the forge—a slotted spoon, a soup ladle, a brand-new hoe.

By the time Nanny showed back up at the spring, the women had predicted that Gabriel would be waiting, and he was. From then on, whenever they could, the two met under the apple tree. They fished and worshipped and danced, always together—Gabriel and Nanny.

"Dolly's boy, Joseph, got sent off to Richmond," Nanny told Gabriel one night. "A six-year-old boy! I held on to Dolly, and we watched the cart haul her son away. I couldn't let her run after him, could I? She has a baby girl still on the breast. If I'd have let Dolly follow after Joseph the way she wanted to do—screamin' and carryin' on—the old colonel's man might have put her in the cart, too."

Gabriel clenched his mouth. *What could Nanny have done?* he asked himself. *What could I have done? Nothing. Nothing any of us can ever do.* He picked up a twig from around the tree. "Then what happened, Nan?"

"I wrapped my arms around her," Nanny told him. "I dragged Dolly off, away to my house, so she wouldn't see. She thrashed all about. I just held on to her, let her dig into me. Look here." Nanny loosened her blouse and showed Gabriel the scratches and cuts along her neck.

He ran his fingers across Nanny's collarbone. Gabriel wondered, if he kissed the marks over and over, might the wounds all disappear? If he held her tight enough, might she forget? "There'll be a scar here," he said.

"I know." Nanny brought her hand to her throat. "I don't mind. Dolly could have clawed all the way to my heart, and I would not have let go of her." Her gaze settled far away, across the meadow to someplace Gabriel could not see.

"The missus stood over us, tellin' Dolly, 'Calm down. Joseph's going to a fine home in South Carolina.' Even the little master cried out, 'Where is Joseph going? Why can't Joseph stay here with me, Mother? Who will play with me now?'"

Nanny rested the bridge of her nose between the braided muscles of Gabriel's arms. She sighed, and he wished he could relieve her suffering.

Sitting there, holding Nanny, Gabriel's boyhood days washed over him, and he let the truth rise up. *I should have seen the lie long before I did*, he thought. *Before Thomas Henry changed. Before Thomas Henry struck me with the man's board, I was like Joseph. A plaything, but a plaything.*

A memory passed through Gabriel's mind. In early childhood, he ate breakfast with Thomas Henry in the great house on many a morning. He slept on the floor in Thomas Henry's bedroom on many a night, too.

One morning when Gabriel and Thomas Henry got caught at the kitchen table with a plate full of cake crumbs, yet no cake before them, Kissey tore into the boys. They had eaten Mr. Prosser's birthday cake — not just one piece between them, not just a piece for each of them, but the entire pound cake.

"What in tarnation happened here?" Kissey had asked. "And before you go tellin' me a lie, Thomas Henry, wipe that sugar from off your chin!" Then Kissey wagged her finger at Gabriel and clucked her tongue. "You ought know better. That's *all* I have to say to *you*." She yanked both children by a hand and dragged them before Mrs. Prosser.

When Kissey told the missus, Ann Prosser licked her thumb and cleaned all evidence from Gabriel's face. First, she addressed Kissey: "Are you not feeding him quite enough?" Then she spoke to Gabriel. "Child, were you very hungry? Is that why you ate the pound cake?"

Gabriel had only followed Thomas Henry, but to Mrs. Prosser he just shrugged. He felt Thomas Henry staring at his back.

Mrs. Prosser squeezed Gabriel's hands. "Today is Mr. Prosser's birthday. Did you know that Kissey fixed that cake up special for your master? I asked her

POUND CAKE
from Mrs. Randolph

WASH the salt from a pound of butter and rub it till it is soft as cream—have ready a pound of flour sifted, one of powdered sugar, and twelve eggs well beaten; put alternately into the butter, sugar, flour, and the froth from the eggs—continuing to beat them together till all the ingredients are in and the cake is quite light: add some grated lemon peel, a nutmeg, and a gill of brandy; butter the pans and bake them. The cakes make an excellent pudding if baked in a large mold and eaten with sugar and wine. They are also excellent when boiled and served up with melted butter, sugar, and wine.

especially to make Mary Randolph's pound cake, and she worked very hard to do so. What do you say for yourself, Gabriel?"

He looked over at the cook. "I liked your cake, Miss Kissey. Would you please make me one for my birthday?"

Mrs. Prosser pretended to scold him. "Now, listen to me, Mister Gabriel: if Kissey baked for everyone at Brookfield, she would hardly have time for anything else. Besides, not everyone here has a birthday. Mr. Prosser wrote yours down in his book, Gabriel, but I'm afraid none of us knows Kissey's, because she was born someplace far away from Brookfield." Mrs. Prosser looked at Kissey. "Do you know your own birthday?" she asked.

"No, missus," Kissey answered, and raised her eyebrows at Gabriel, warning him to keep his mouth quiet.

"See there?" Mrs. Prosser stroked Gabriel's cheek. "No, love, cakes are just for the family." She gently pushed Gabriel away and nodded for Kissey to take him. "I think you and Thomas Henry have had enough playtime today. Why don't you run out to the south field now? They might need you to bring water; it's unmercifully hot this afternoon."

That evening, after Mr. Prosser's birthday dinner, Kissey fetched Gabriel from the quarter. "Young master askin' for Gabriel. He's scared to sleep by hisself, again," Kissey said.

Gabriel felt relieved that Thomas Henry still wanted to be with him.

When Gabriel reached the great house and saw Thomas Henry sitting and waiting on the top porch step, he waved and ran up the stairs, glad in a way that he would sleep in the house, away from the bugs and away from Dog, who would most likely come home to the quarter with muddy legs, stinking of the marsh from her late-night hunt. But, most of all, he was glad things were good again with Thomas Henry. *We are like brothers. Everyone says so.*

He had a new song to teach Thomas Henry and decided to teach his friend that night. *We'll sing in the dark, like always,* he had thought.

Yet Thomas Henry had run into the house without a word for Gabriel.

Inside, Kissey put both boys in crisp linen sleeping shirts. To keep the mosquitoes at bay, she draped Thomas Henry's bed with netting that hung from the ceiling.

For Gabriel, she made a pallet on the floor.

Gabriel loved Kissey's pallets, and this one felt extra plump. When Kissey bent down to tuck the sheet under Gabriel's chin, he put his hands on her round moon face and pulled her ear close to his mouth. "You can have my birthday, Miss Kissey," he whispered. "We can share."

Kissey swiped at Gabriel's nose. She pushed the tip of her thumb out between her fingers. "Thumbkin got your sniffer." Kissey wagged the tip of her peeking-out thumb, and this made Gabriel giggle.

"Take your leave now, Kissey," Thomas Henry said.

Kissey pecked Gabriel's forehead, and once she closed the door, he snuggled down deep into the pallet to hide away from the bright-white light from the window, imposing itself on the darkness. The moon pierced through his closed eyes, so he pulled the sheet up over his head. He let the night hold him, and the night returned him to his own natural breath.

He set his hands on his belly and felt his clasped fingers open wide apart when he inhaled and come back, touching, when he let his breath go. His even and steady breath drew him into the invisible world inside, where he was always just Gabriel.

When he had about reached the tunnel that would take him through sleep, to the place where he could be his whole and true self, Thomas Henry jolted him back awake and aware of the hard floor.

"After she sent you off to the field, Mother wore my tail out today, Gabriel, for eating Father's cake. This is your fault, and you should have spoken up for me." Thomas Henry rolled back over and leaned down to Gabriel. "You're Mother's pet. Haven't you noticed?"

Gabriel poked his head out from under the sheet. "I'm no one's pet. I'm Gabriel."

"Mother should have whipped you worse than she whipped me. Of course you're her pet. Who else would teach you to read?"

Gabriel burrowed deep in the covers so that he couldn't see Thomas Henry anymore. He could still smell Kissey's kitchen scent from where she had tucked the bedclothes under his chin. The lingering of grease and flour and corn, mixed with Kissey's skin, made Gabriel wish Kissey would come and take him back to Ma in the quarter. Even from the great house, he could hear Dog baying in the forest, and he wondered if Old Major had gotten a squirrel or a rabbit or a nasty opossum.

Thomas Henry turned his back to Gabriel. He said over his shoulder, "You just remember this: Mother likes you so well because I like you, and if I didn't, I might tell her all sorts of stories about the trouble you cause; then do you know what she'd do?"

"No." Gabriel's stomach turned queasy.

"She would tell Father to sell you, and you'd be sent away from Brookfield, just on her word. You'd never again see your mother or your brothers or Kissey or me. One day, Gabriel, I will be the master of Brookfield. I do whatever I want; just remember that."

This is my home, too, Gabriel thought at the time, and he rose up from his place on the floor. He went to find Kissey so she could console him.

Now, all these years later, it was Gabriel doing the consoling. He put his arms around Nanny, who wept over Joseph and Dolly. He recalled how Thomas Henry had tossed around in his downy bed after the threat. Then he understood; Thomas Henry had only ever loved him in the way that privileged people love their possessions.

The conviction that had been growing in his heart for some years, which burned only stronger since he'd come back from Jacob's forge, formed clearly in him now: *I am my own master. Gabriel belongs only to Gabriel.*

CHAPTER TWELVE
April 1795

A MONTH, a year, then two years, passed. People came and went, were bought and sold, from Young's, from Wilkinson's, and from Brookfield. In every season, Gabriel let Nanny cry for a child, for a mother, for herself. One Sunday, Nanny's tears stopped.

"What happens if I've used up all the sorrow God gave me?" Nanny asked Gabriel. She lamented the wall enclosing her heart. "I'd hardly remember the looks of my own sisters if I didn't see my own face in the creek." She leaned against Gabriel's strong arms.

He held her close enough to him so that her heart could keep its mournful beat with his. "It's all right to look at your own hurting, Nan. You're safe with me," he said. His face burned. *Makin' a fool of myself.*

Nanny took in a deep breath, then blurted out to him, "Even knowin' what happens to a family . . . if I could choose any man in the world to make my child, I would choose you, Gabriel." She confessed and then sucked in her breath, trying to recapture those words.

She broke from Gabriel's hold and ran from the green-apple tree, down through the greener hillside, toward the spring. In but a few strides, Gabriel caught up and took her hand.

"Is that an invitation, Nan?" Gabriel finally asked. "Or just a thought?"

Nanny answered him by kissing the scar on the inside of his forearm, a mark shaped like the scythe the people used every day in Colonel Wilkinson's field.

He rubbed his thumb across the raised bean of skin and explained. "My first good burn. From forging my own hammer. I needed a longer handle and a heavier head than what my teacher gave me, so he told me to make my own, and I did." He opened his hand to show her more. "My second good burn—forging a rosette for a gate. I thought I had doused the thing in water, but I hadn't."

She bent her face over the delicate brown flower

singed into the pale pink well of Gabriel's palm. Nanny kissed that scar, too, until Gabriel let go a deep, contented sigh.

She touched the old gash on his forehead, the one made by Thomas Henry. "Not a burn," Nanny said.

"No, it happened when I was a boy."

They walked beside each other in silence along the hillside. He couldn't help but let himself daydream a future day, one when Nanny and he might go down to the brook, a free man and his free wife. By then, he would have told her all the stories of all his scars and marks—his missing front teeth, the long gash down his brow, and the deep marks across his back. He imagined a night when he would have Nan all to himself. On that first night, he would let her explore all of these places with her eyes and her hands and her kisses. Whether scars of his trade or marks of the lie, he would give Nanny the whole of what he carried in his heart and on his person.

Gabriel smelled the promise of plum and apple and pear come wafting up from Young's orchard. He linked his arm with hers. Neither of them heard the final notes of the last hymn rise up from the preachment at the spring. Gabriel stopped walking and pulled Nanny close to him.

She pressed the bridge of her nose into the contour of his shoulder. "I see the life I want," she said, "but how can it come to be?"

Gabriel had no answer for her. In just a few minutes, she would be gone from him for another week. He pulled her tighter into his arms and rested his chin on her head. "I been knowing you a long time, Nan," he said.

All of the forest seemed to recognize what passed from his heart to hers. The canopy let enter a golden glow, shining out from the clouds and directly down onto them. The smallest of yellow warblers and its fellow songbirds darted out of the creek's soft edges; their voices filled Gabriel with hope.

He shook his head and smiled.

Nanny pushed on his arm. "What?"

He twirled her the way he did when they danced in the forest. "Just thinking. Wondering 'bout how our child might turn out to be."

"Be like half you and half me." Nanny let herself go free of Gabriel's hold and ran to catch up with Colonel Wilkinson's other women. The sunset's fading and their friends' leaving reminded them that there was always work left undone.

"Nan!" His words and his thoughts parted ways, both chasing after her. *Will you marry me?* he had meant to say, but Nanny was too far—gone away back up the hill. Now Gabriel knew something else about himself. *I belong to Gabriel, yes. And I belong, also, to Nanny.*

CHAPTER THIRTEEN
April 1795

HE RAN BACK to Brookfield. *Nanny loves me, and I am different,* Gabriel thought.

What did she say, exactly? He tried to recall.

Dog greeted him at the apple tree. She jumped and bounced, begging Gabriel to turn back and take her night-hunting in the forest. He patted the hound on her flat head and caught Nanny's words by the tail before they slipped away down the creek.

"If I could choose any man . . . I would choose you."

He stopped beneath his tree to imagine his Nanny, again and again. Dog curled up at Gabriel's feet, content to groan herself to sleep.

Was Nanny smiling when she told me? No, she looked sad. But then she reached for my hand. Did she say my name? Did I squeeze her hand back, or did she pull us along the hillside? Why didn't I kiss her on the lips?

He recounted every step of their walk until he could recall only how the creek and Nanny's face were alight with the gold of the sky, the flowers, and the spring birds.

The whole world is different, he thought. *I need a plan.*

He roused Dog. "Come on, girl. We got work to do."

He knew then that he *would* marry Nanny, and that he would love her forever. Now he needed only to figure out how they could have the free life they imagined. Even though it was Sunday night, Gabriel itched to get to the forge. He always had plenty of smithing to do, but now he had a new problem to solve.

In the back corner of the forge, away from the hearth and out of reach of the anvil, repair work for Kissey and Ma and Mrs. Prosser waited on Gabriel, waited on a day like this one, when there were no horses to shoe, no broken-down buggies or carriages to interrupt him.

Broken pots and pot handles, trivets and andirons, gave Gabriel seamless hours of Sunday-night work to

1795, BROOKFIELD SHOP JOBS

April 1st
18 nails
1 nut to buggy screw
1 bolt and nut to the carriage
2 braces to a wheel barrough
pointing 1 double plough
nailing in old shoes on the bay mare
laying a grubbing hoe
a kitchen tribbet
peacing a prong to a pitchfork
mending a hook to a gate

— 2nd
2 pair of new shoes for Thomas Henry's horse
mending a garding rake and teeth to it
mending a pitchfork
2 screws and nuts
2 links and 2 hooks to a chain
laying the eye to a grubbing hoe
1 hook to a stretcher chain
1 pair of new shoes for the bay mare
a peace of iron on a saddle

think and plan. In his smithy in the woods, there was no master smith to wake, no setting up but for himself. Even so, Gabriel started his work with the anvil beat.

Ping, ping, ping. Ping, ping, ping.

Gabriel pinched off the broken handle from Kissey's teakettle. He pulled on the bellows to make fire, calling forth a great sigh from the great leather lung. He thought of his own torn-apart family.

Maybe Pa messed up, talking about everybody being free. What if Pa had hired out and worked to free Ma and me and my brothers? Would Pa still be with us? Would he and Ma be free? Would all of us?

Clang, clang, clang. Ping. Clang, clang, clang. Ping. By now, Gabriel knew other men—blacksmiths, coopers, and carpenters—who had made their own money doing extra work, hiring out in the city or around the countryside. Some even saved up to buy freedom for their wives.

I can read and write; I can count and hammer. Just like the washerwomen told me that day by the creek: Hire myself out and make my own money. Work much as I want and buy what I want. All I want is Nanny. Make enough money to free Nanny. Simple. I will deliver Nanny and, maybe, myself.

Clang, clang, clang. Ping.

———

Now Gabriel realized that to be truly with Nanny, the way a man wants to be with his woman, first he must leave her. He must go and make enough money to buy her freedom. Later, he would worry about buying his own.

Clang, clang, clang. Ping.

If the old colonel owns Nanny, our children will belong to the old colonel. So says the law. If Nanny owns Nanny, our children will belong only to themselves. So says the law.

Gabriel knew that his value in the marketplace would bring top pay, and he knew that his master, Mr. Prosser, was even thirstier for cash than land. While Virginia law allowed Mr. Prosser to rent Gabriel to another man, the Commonwealth forbade Gabriel from moving about, hiring out on his own. Even so, such practice was common among skilled slaves like Gabriel and greedy men like Mr. Prosser.

Gabriel knew of no other man who could match his own talent or his own strength. How he wished he had listened to the laundresses from the beginning.

Clang, clang, clang. Ping.

No more time to waste. I'll hire out here in Henrico. I'll work in the city and all over the countryside for smiths or planters or even carpenters. Wherever a job can be found, I'll work seven days a week—all day, all night—to save for

Nanny. Shoeing horses, mending fences, digging on the canal or forging bullets—I'll work for Nan. When I have saved up, I'll make Nanny my wife, then set her free.

He dunked the repaired handle in the water barrel to set its shape. The next morning, with his plan well established in his own mind, Gabriel took the mended teakettle to Kissey. In turn, the grateful cook arranged a private visit for Gabriel with Mr. Prosser.

Kissey, showing gray at her temples but still well in control of the household, showed Gabriel to Mr. Prosser's counting room. Even after she closed the door to give them privacy, Gabriel could see Kissey's starched black dress hem pressed against the gap at the bottom rail of the door.

Kissey's looking after me, he thought. *If my talk with Mr. Prosser turns bad, Kissey will interrupt with urgent business.*

Neither Gabriel nor the cook need to have worried. Mr. Prosser hungrily agreed that Gabriel could hire himself out as he pleased. The two settled on a monthly allotment for Gabriel to turn over to Brookfield—anything above that, Gabriel could keep. They both understood that their agreement was neither binding nor legal.

With this first part of his plan in place, Gabriel set

about finding good work in the countryside. Jupiter and Isaac were known to seek out the mildest of masters when hiring out, and neither would work for a man of cruel repute. A man's manners meant nothing to Gabriel; what mattered was the job and the pay. He often said to his friends, "There is no such thing as a kind or gentle master. Besides, liberty is my only master and money its only means."

Gabriel imagined what he would tell Nanny's master, the old colonel, in three, maybe four years. *"I am here to manumit my wife," I'll say.*

"Manumit," Gabriel said. "Our free and united life starts today."

By the next Friday, Gabriel had arranged to hire on at a shop in Caroline County, twenty-five miles north of Brookfield. First he walked to the old colonel's place to tell Nanny good-bye.

CHAPTER FOURTEEN
May 1795

GABRIEL FOUND NANNY weeding the garden she shared with the other women. He crouched low in the brush at the edge of Nanny's quarter and spied on her hoeing the hard patch of ground that the colonel let them work. In Nanny's hands, the earth seemed eager to grow beans and peas, onions and okra, and squashes of all kinds.

He loved how Nanny made her garden different from the others. Where a boulder rose from the earth, Nanny worked around it. Gabriel had once offered to bring some men to dig up the rock so she could set her rows straight, but Nanny had refused.

"Makes a good place for me to sit and watch," she had told him. "I like to use the earth how the earth wants to be used."

So Nanny's garden flourished in patches and circles and swirls, following the contours of the earth. Where the ground stayed wet, she set out thirsty plants—melons and cantaloupes. Where the sun would not relent, she put the light-loving okra and tomatoes.

Across the glade, he watched her until he needed to touch her, then he called out, "Nan! I've brought something for you."

Nanny dropped her hoe and ran toward him.

Gabriel held out a sack. "For you, hardworking woman. I know you need fire to sew by at night."

She peeked inside, then clasped her hands. "Pine knots!" She breathed in the pine aroma. "There's enough in here to last for weeks." Nanny kissed him on the cheek.

He hadn't expected this kiss, not in front of everyone. His face flushed at the warmth of her lips on his face, and he said the first thing he thought. "I've been gathering pine knots my whole entire life. Ma used to would tell anybody, 'Gabriel knows which ones burn long and bright. He must smell the resin.' I reckon she was right, too." He unlaced a raccoon dangling from his belt and handed the carcass to Nanny. "This, too. For you."

With Dog's help, he had found and killed two coons in their sleep. He had given one to the hound for a job well done, then had sent Dog on back to Brookfield. Gabriel told Nanny, "Too easy to not get some good meat for you on the way over. You'll have to do the cleaning."

Nanny took the sack and the kill. "Bringing me gifts on a Friday afternoon? Show me your permit, hammerman." She teased him. "Mmmm, I know. Mister Gabriel does up his own passes!"

He reached into his pocket and handed her the paper that Prosser's man had written, permitting him to travel the road to his job in Caroline.

She looked at the pass and touched the words. "Is my name on this paper? Show me where."

"Won't find your name on this paper. See this word? It says *Caroline*."

Nanny screwed up her face. "You got another girl?"

Gabriel laughed. "I got something important to say, Nan. So just listen."

Nanny nodded. "You always look up at the sky when you start tellin' tales. I'll know if you're lyin'," she warned him.

The other women in the garden stopped working then. One by one, they paused their shovels and hoes to listen to Gabriel.

He cleared his throat. "Ever since we talked at the spring about making a life, I've been planning. You won't see me at the spring tomorrow . . . maybe not for weeks or even months. I'm going to Caroline County to hire out. Solomon will keep the shop running. If you need a thing, you go see him. You're the only girl, Nan. You understand?"

She shook her head and pleaded, "Don't go off and leave me. The other day at the spring—I shouldn't have said a word about havin' children. My feelin's are just feelin's. I can put them back. Please, don't go. I—"

"Hush, now." Gabriel put his finger to Nanny's lips. "Would you choose me? That true what you said, Nanny?"

She lowered her voice. "The truest."

"Then I choose you, too. I'm a man, Nanny. Not Prosser's slave man. *Your* man. Be my wife?" He gave her one final present, a hammered-out thin silver circle strung into a necklace with a length of twine. He remembered how when they were last together, he later regretted what he had left undone, so before she could speak a word, he took Nanny's face in his hands. She shut her eyes, and he kissed her.

Her friends had all dropped their tools by now.

Gabriel smiled at the circle of women gathered around Nan. He wanted them all to hear how much he loved this woman. "I'll work everywhere, anywhere, and for anyone willing to hire me. Give Mr. Prosser his share—how we agreed—and when I've saved enough to buy your freedom, you can start that life we imagined at the creek. After you're free, then our children will be free. So says Virginia."

When Nanny said nothing, Gabriel looked to the women for help. One of them nudged Nanny closer to him, but she remained silently weeping.

"Well, I just come down here to tell you my plan." He picked up a stick and squatted down to write in the dirt. "There," he said, then added, "I don't need your name written on any pass." He tapped his chest. "*Nanny.* Your name's written here." Gabriel turned to leave.

"Wait!" Nanny finally spoke. She reached out and rested her hand over Gabriel's heart. "I'll be here, Gabriel."

He left Wilkinson's place by the north trail through the forest. Even once the jays had stopped cawing and the squirrels had quit chirring after him, Nanny stood on her garden rock, waving. Then she bent to the ground and traced the letters in the dirt, first with her finger and then with the same stick that Gabriel had used to write her name: *Nanny.*

CHAPTER FIFTEEN
November 1795

IN THE FALL, well after the last harvest, Gabriel obtained a weekend pass and put aside his work. He rushed back to Henrico, tracking through the woods along a narrow rise in the land, toting his best tools, those hammers and tongs and wedges that he could not work without. He hurried back to see Nanny.

Gabriel did not need to keep a list of reasons why he loved her. His love for Nan was in everything within and around him. When he walked through the forest, he heard Nanny singing, not the wren. When his stomach churned with hunger, he didn't crave Ma's food or even Kissey's, just a simple meal of Nanny's making. The place on his chest where Nanny had last touched him burned for her. The bare November trees let him see far down the ridge, and for miles he told himself, *Almost home. Almost home to Nan.*

When, at last, the earth's slope turned low and flat, he bayed for Dog. "Ah-oo. Ah-oo." He called for the hound, and in the distance the dog called back.

He walked for another half mile, until he reached the Chickahominy Swamp. There, Gabriel sat down on the thick roots of a great old cypress to wait for Dog and to think of Nanny. Gabriel was tired. More than anything, he wanted to rest his head in Nanny's lap. *I'll shut my eyes, rest here a minute. Just till Dog finds me.*

The sun was setting when Dog's wet nose nudged Gabriel awake. The air had grown cool, and the forest floor had turned moist. The hound walked with him back to Brookfield. On the way, the pair of them filled Gabriel's belt with meat enough for Nanny and Ma. He gave Dog her fair share for her part in the hunt.

When he reached Brookfield, Gabriel checked in with Prosser's man, then slipped away past the apple tree, down the hill, and into Nanny's arms. On his first night back, they skipped the gathering in the woods, and he started teaching Nanny the letters. She wanted to learn to read and write.

By the pine-knot fire and the light of one small candle, he took up a stick and wrote *A* on the dirt floor. "*Apple*," said Gabriel. "Like our tree."

"*A. Apple*," Nanny repeated, and copied in the dirt.

"Now, *B. Bear.* Ever seen a bear in the forest, Nan?"

At *C*, he felt Nanny's hand on his knee. He thought to get up and toss another knot onto the fire, but the heat from Nanny's palm kept him still. "This one is called *C*. Say *C*," he said.

Nanny brought her hand up to the back of Gabriel's neck, and she kissed his ear. "I already said *C*." She set her cheek on his shoulder.

He closed his eyes and tried to say the next letter, but he could only want more Nanny. More of her touch on his leg and more of her breath on his arm. Gabriel turned his face to Nanny's; his mouth nearly touched hers. He had only to part his lips, and Nanny's lips would be right there. When he dared to reach out just a bit more, she kissed him back. But such a rare and sweet stolen night by the firelight was not nearly enough time for them.

Gabriel spent the next three years working throughout the region, making Nanny's freedom money. Every week, every month, every year, brought them closer to their dream. When he turned twenty-two, Gabriel could wait no longer. With almost all of Nanny's freedom money saved up, Gabriel went back up to the great house.

CHAPTER SIXTEEN
October 1798

*Thomas Prosser Daily Journal —
Brookfield 1798*

*Tuesday, October 2 — Fine morning. I feel quite
unwell. Will remain at home today. Thomas
Henry went into town with the waggon.
Sent a load of hay to sell. T. H. requested
of me $100. As I did not have it to give,
gave him 30. All hands gathered corn.*

Wednesday, October 3 — Very fine weather. Thomas Henry did not return last evening. I feel quite unwell still and have a fever. Hands commenced seeding wheat. The Old Major no better. Sent for doctor.

Thursday, October 4 — Fine weather. Continued seeding wheat. The doctor did not leave here until 10 o'clock this morning. He thinks James, the Old Major, dangerously ill. I feel very unwell this morning. May try to go to town tomorrow.

Friday, October 5 — Weather turned cold abruptly. Feel very weak, so much so that I have not been able to go out of the house. Sorry to hear Kissey so unwell. Thomas Henry took the carriage to town. Gave him $0. The fever, the villain, took James during the night.

GABRIEL had new business at the great house. Having saved what he thought nearly enough to free Nanny, he would now seek Mr. Prosser's permission to marry her. He thought he had best keep his freedom plan to himself, at least until Nan and he were husband and wife. He knew if he straightaway told Mr. Prosser of his intention to manumit Nanny, the old man might withhold his blessing.

Do this right and we're one step closer. After we jump the broom, then I'll go see Colonel Wilkinson about buying away Nanny.

In his years of working and saving, Gabriel had thought only of how to get what he wanted. The money in his pocket made him feel powerful. Powerful enough to believe.

We'll live in the city. I'll work with Jacob awhile, till I save my own freedom money. Then I'll make my own shop, and Nanny can have a room for her sewing.

But a vicious fever had torn through the city and the countryside. From Brookfield, the cruel monster had taken away Old Major and other elders from the quarter and even those littlest ones, born weak from the start. Ma and Kissey were lying out in their huts, too low to work, too ill to worry about Prosser's man. Dog, Old Major's friend for life, was lying out, too, by the graves. She sat atop the mound of earth covering the place where she'd watched them set Old Major in the ground. No one could get near Dog now, not even Gabriel. Her righteous, ferocious self had come around fully, back to wild.

On Saturday, when Gabriel went up to see Mr. Prosser, Venus showed him to the counting room, not Kissey.

When Gabriel asked about Dog, Venus just shook her head and clicked her tongue. "She went along her whole life just playactin' nice, I guess. She figure without Old Major she got no chance. Got nothin'. Gone back to her true colors, I reckon. Snarlin' and showin' those nasty teeth. Hurt somebody now, for sure."

When Mr. Prosser closed the door, Venus took Kissey's old place. The planter invited Gabriel to sit, but Gabriel remained standing. A fine log fire roared high in the fireplace. Mr. Prosser adjusted his chair and draped a wool throw across his shoulders.

"What's your business with me today, Gabriel? I haven't much time."

Gabriel could see Venus waiting there on the other side of the closed door. Her dress hem did not calm him in the same way Kissey's would have, but he smiled at her trying to do him right. Seeing her there helped him gather his nerve.

"Sir, I'm here asking your permission to marry Colonel Wilkinson's Nanny," he said.

Mr. Prosser leaned back in his chair and wrinkled his brow. Tears of sweat collected along the planter's upper lip. The master looked ample worried, but Gabriel had ample time to wait. He let Mr. Prosser search his face. He let the master take in each scar and hoped he'd recall the story of every mark. Gabriel left his lips just apart to show the gaps in his mouth, so Prosser could see and remember.

Gabriel rested his gaze on the mantel and on the oil painting of a young Thomas Henry standing beside a dog who was not Dog. He wondered if the portrait would hang there for years or decades or even centuries to come. He wondered if future Prossers and kin might say, "That's little Thomas Henry Prosser; he's the one who squandered the family fortune."

He pondered what surname he might choose for his own family when he and Nan were free to adorn their own mantel and their own names in any way they pleased.

"Your presence here this morning is unsettling to

me, Gabriel," the old man said at last. "I dreamed a terrible dream last night. All morning, I've been given over to a great anxiety. Sit."

Gabriel took the wing chair facing Mr. Prosser and the doorway. He heard Venus rustling in the foyer— her way of warning him to keep still and ready.

"I take seriously my responsibility to provide for the care and protection of all my family here at Brookfield. Have I not been generous with you ever since you can recall?" Mr. Prosser asked him. "Are you not happy, Gabriel?"

He knew what Mr. Prosser meant by "family." Mr. Prosser often called Gabriel's people family, though he had never known Mr. Prosser to tie his wife or his son naked to a tree limb, then leave them lying out in winter to wait for a whipping.

In the counting room, Gabriel's heart and mind worked to one accord. He had come seeking Mr. Prosser's mercy, not his wrath, so he answered, "I am most happy when I'm with Nanny. Sir."

Mr. Prosser laughed to himself. "Ah, yes. You've come for a gift!" The planter man coughed once, then twice, and with the third he gave in to a violent hacking fit. Venus slipped into the room and placed a glass of water in the master's trembling hand. The girl nodded for Gabriel to hurry with his request, then left the two men alone again.

"I've been loving Nanny since I first saw her when I first went to Richmond."

"I knew you visited Wilkinson's at night lately." Mr. Prosser crossed, then uncrossed, his ankles and leaned forward. "But tell me, what do you think about Venus? I have long hoped you would take Venus."

Gabriel shook his head *no* before Mr. Prosser could finish speaking. He looked to the door, thankful some other business had pulled Venus away. Still, he softened his voice before he spoke so that she would not hear. "Thank you, sir. I love my Nan, and besides, Venus is too trifling a woman for me."

Mr. Prosser leaned his head against the chair back and groaned. So much time passed that Gabriel cleared his throat to try and rouse the master from sleep.

Venus entered the room again and startled Mr. Prosser awake.

"Yes, yes," the planter said. "I give you my permission. I'll speak to Wilkinson on your behalf, though I expect the old colonel will take no issue. He's getting the better part here. You must know I'll have no claim on any increase from this marriage." Mr. Prosser picked up his pen to write their agreement in the book, then set it down again. "Venus, I can't get warm today. Send Old Major in to tend to this fire."

Venus and Gabriel exchanged glances. "Old Major passed over, Marse. Gone home now," said Venus.

Mr. Prosser rubbed his eyes. "Did I not just see him there at my window? Well, I'm tired and nervous today." The master sighed. "I need a good strong cup of coffee. Or some soup. Now, tell me, how is your mother?"

"Comin' 'long, sir. Mam be back up here to the house before long," Venus answered.

"Good, good. I miss having Kissey near." He sank deep into his chair, then remembered Gabriel. "I'll do your bidding with Wilkinson. Are we finished?"

"Thank you," Gabriel said. Then he rushed to add, "Venus here, she loves Mr. Burton's Isaac, sir, and it's a known fact he loves her back. Isaac's a good, strong man and will care for her."

Before Gabriel could wink at Venus and slip out of the counting room, Mr. Prosser grabbed Gabriel by the wrist. "Wait."

"Sir?"

"I dreamed of your damned father last night. He came to my bed drenched by rain. Laughing." Mr. Prosser described the ghostly encounter. "I asked what business he had with me, then his face became yours. On waking this morning, I prevailed upon Venus to check the floor for dampness, to see if he had come back and haunted me in the night."

Gabriel envisioned Pa's bony face. Even now, he met up with Pa every night in his sleep. He had often wondered if he would speak a single word or simply fall into Pa's embrace when they would finally reunite, way up yonder. He wanted so badly to tell his father, *Pa, I'm going to marry Nanny at Young's spring. I'm going to set my Nan free.*

He said to himself, *We'll hold hands when we jump the broom. Three times, then she'll be my wife. Forever, Pa. Like you and Ma, forever.*

"I also dreamed of my father in the night," Gabriel said, and ran from the counting room. Mr. Prosser had kept the room so hot, now Gabriel felt dizzy and out of breath. Outside, he leaned against the cold, white wood planks of the great house, then he set off past the quarter to Young's spring to meet Nanny.

He knew she would be waiting. Seeing him there, smiling his snaggletooth smile at the top of the hill, Nanny would come running toward him. He would call out, *My bride, my bride,* over and over when he saw her blue skirt hiked up to give her long legs room to sprint up the hill. She would jump into his arms when she reached him, then he would swing her around and around and love her right there on the still side of the hill. Afterward, Nan would complain about being cold. He would bring all of her into his lap until she felt warm again.

But when Gabriel did reach the apple tree, he changed his mind. The smell of fallen, fermenting fruit longing to return to the earth bade him turn around back to the quarter. *Nan will wait.*

He took the last three ready apples from his tree — one for Nanny, one for himself, and one for Ma. *I'll visit Ma first,* he decided. He bit into the fruit without polishing it first on his shirt. He knew the superstition about unclean apples, and he didn't care.

Gabriel, scared of nothin', Ma always would say. He could hear her scolding him good. *Now, Gabriel, wipe off that apple, or you askin' for trouble from the devil hisself.*

Let Satan come on, and Mr. Prosser, too, Gabriel thought. *I'm goin' to marry my Nan!*

The whole way back to Ma's hut, Gabriel planned what he would say, how he would tell Ma. He wanted to bring her this small gift of the last apple of the season while she lay suffering in the clutches of the fever.

The news about a wedding would ease her spirit. *Nanny will wait for me till I get back from telling Ma.*

His ma was resting, curled up in Pa's bed. Venus or Mrs. Prosser or someone else had brought quilts down from the house and laid them three deep across her. Gabriel sniffed the top one for cornmeal or lavender to tell who had been caring for his mother. The bedclothes smelled of bacon. *Venus,* he thought. *She's all right, that Venus. All right after all.*

Ma had yet to stir or roll over. He dunked his kerchief in the water bucket, wrung it out, and draped the cool indigo scrap cloth around the back of Ma's neck.

"Ma," Gabriel said. "I got good news. Mr. Prosser agreed. I'm marrying Nanny."

She groaned a little.

"Nobody knows yet, Ma, but you and me: I've about saved up all Nanny's free money. Your grandchildren will be free and Virginia born, Ma."

She still hadn't moved, so Gabriel tried to tease her by saying what Ma always said to him when she had big news. "Now, that's what I know. What do you know?"

Ma managed to roll over and reached for Gabriel. Her lips were dry and cracked. One suffering eye, swollen purple and protruding onto her cheek, was already gone on ahead to seek the best way home. And the other, still tender and searching, fixed Gabriel. "Where's your pa?" Ma whispered.

"Shhh," Gabriel said. "That fever got you seeing things good. That's what a fever does. Pa's gone on. A long time now. You remember?"

"Pa gone already?" Ma looked lost in a place she should have known well. "I was just talkin' to him. He asked me what kind of trouble you makin'. Asked about your lady, too. Pa gone already?"

Then Gabriel knew for sure. *Only the dying see the dead.* He folded her frail hand around the apple.

Ma brought the green apple to her nose and inhaled deep. "Little boy, you remember how you liked to climb? You remember how you'd shinny up, way up the tippy-top, up that tree? You liked to leave your brother behind and stay all alone up there."

He kissed her forehead.

"'I can see all the way to Colonel Wilkinson's,' you would tell me. And what would I say to you?"

Gabriel closed his eyes and squeezed her hand. He shook his head no to stop her from dying, but she persisted.

"Tell me, son. You remember? Tell me, what would I say to you?"

He gave in. "You never told me to get down. You'd ask me, 'That's all the far you see, child? Just to the colonel's place? Come on, now, how far can you see, angel-boy? To the city, to the market, to the sea?'" Gabriel laughed at the memory, then told her, "But Wilkinson's is 'bout far as I need to see these days. Only got eyes for Nanny, Ma. Ma?"

Gabriel never made it to Wilkinson's place that day. He stayed with Ma through the night, until sunrise, guarding her body until he felt sure her spirit had reached its true home and reunited with Pa.

When he went up to tell Venus of Ma's passing over, he learned that, though Kissey had, thankfully, survived the fever, the great house was in mourning. With Mr. Prosser's death, the care and protection of all the people was conveyed to Thomas Henry.

Gabriel, Solomon, and Martin buried Ma beside Old Major. The folks who were well or recovered enough came to pay their respects, and they knelt beside her grave while the boys recited psalms and while each one wondered to himself what kind of man could go on without his mother.

By then, Dog had become a hideous sight to behold from her own grieving heart. Thomas Henry declared her a threat to Brookfield and prevailed on Gabriel to take Mr. Prosser's pistol to Dog's temple. Instead, Gabriel drove Dog deep into the swamp, but he wouldn't pull the trigger on Dog. Ever.

"Go on," he told her. "You're free to be anywhere but Brookfield." Then he felt the giant crater in his heart where Ma used to be. He said to Dog, "I know just how you feel, girl. Go on, now. Free to go anywhere but home."

When Gabriel told Thomas Henry the truth—that he had run the hound off and set her free—the twenty-two-year-old new lord of Brookfield erupted. "Insolent!" he called Gabriel. In return for Gabriel's defying him, Thomas Henry refused to honor the late Mr. Prosser's promise to Gabriel.

"Besides," Thomas Henry said, "Father wrote nothing in his book regarding permission for you to marry Wilkinson's Nanny. I desire that you marry Venus instead."

Once, Gabriel had loved Thomas Henry and preferred Thomas Henry's company to that of his brothers, but now he could not even stomach the sweet, pampered smell of him. He recalled how Ma had told him once, "Workin' hard never been good enough to set a person free or keep a man with his family. Now, that's what I know; what do you know?"

What Gabriel knew was that even a constant flow of money would never satisfy Thomas Henry. Mr. Prosser had willed his son plenty of land, bequeathed him fifty hands, and yet left his son penniless. To get what he wanted, to get what he was promised, to get his fair share, Gabriel decided to withhold from hiring out until Thomas Henry agreed to his marriage to Nan.

Show him what I'm worth. Let his pocket feel empty of my earnings. If working hard's not good enough for Thomas Henry to give me what I want, then I won't work at all.

Prosser's man summoned Gabriel to the forge, but Gabriel would not yield, so he was ordered beaten, whipped, and strung up.

CHAPTER SEVENTEEN
September 1799

GABRIEL WITHSTOOD Thomas Henry's wickedness, but Brookfield hardly withstood the new master's mismanagement and neglect. For Gabriel, the year was barbaric. He never thought of running, because of his love for Nanny. Finally, due to the urging of Mrs. Ann Prosser and the dwindling of Brookfield's funds, Thomas Henry relented, and, for a second time, Gabriel was granted permission to marry Nan.

Kin from all around the countryside—Henrico, Hanover, Caroline, and Richmond—were fixing to gather for the nuptials. Mrs. Prosser donated faded blue chintz and a strip of frayed lace toward a new dress for Nanny. Jacob Kent gave Gabriel an old black velvet overcoat when he heard the news. Jupiter promised he would wash his shirt and dry it in the sunshine. Solomon joked that he would gladly take a wife, too, if only Jupiter would also wash out his pants. Now all Gabriel needed was a pig to barbecue for the wedding feast.

Jupiter knew just where to find one.

Solomon and Jupiter accompanied Gabriel to Absalom Johnson's farm for the securing of Nanny's wedding pig. Isaac refused to go along. At the time, Jupiter was hired out to Johnson on land rented from Colonel Wilkinson. Jupiter knew the farm well— where spiders hid from the light, where the best pig slept, and where Johnson napped in the late afternoon. Solomon went to watch out, to create a diversion should the need arise.

By the letter of the law, Absalom Johnson's pig was not Gabriel's to take, though everyone in Henrico embraced the more pliable spirit of the law. Out in the country, moderation abided when livestock went missing. If no man got *caught* stealing, the theft was most often overlooked, but bunglers had best beware.

In the broad light of day, Jupiter slipped under the split-rail fence. He dove for the fattest pig and handed the prize across the fence to Gabriel. The boys congratulated themselves at the easy pickings, but the boys celebrated too soon.

Gabriel did not run but walked from Johnson's barnyard with the pig under his arm. Looking down the wrong end of the lane, Solomon missed Absalom Johnson coming around the back side of the barn. Jupiter didn't see him, nor did Gabriel. The red-haired man—a newcomer to Henrico—possessed no land of his own but possessed of his own a temper, an ego, and something to prove. With cursing and flailing and a high-pitched squeal, Johnson pursued Gabriel and the hog.

The farmer called out after Gabriel, "Thief! Thief!" and ordered Gabriel to set down the pig. When confronted, Gabriel tried to persuade Johnson to consider the animal a small gift and invited the farmer to the upcoming nuptials.

Johnson only yelled louder, this time yelling, "Damned thief!"

Gabriel held fast to the hog. "A fair trade," he said, and then suggested Johnson consider the swine repayment in full for the calf taken from Brookfield by Johnson's own bondmen just last Saturday.

Everyone knows who took that steer from us last week,

Gabriel thought. *Even now half a Brookfield calf hangs in Johnson's smokehouse.*

The farmer laughed at Gabriel, a slave bargaining with a man. Johnson paid his rent to old Colonel Wilkinson in pork so had his own plans for the pig. He had plans for Gabriel, too.

Only just then did Gabriel consider that the hog he held might be anything other than eaten and enjoyed on the day he married Nanny. "Let us go, and I'll let go the pig," he said, too late.

He was thinking about Nanny—not court or jail or the gallows—when Johnson lunged at him. He was thinking, *Nanny might rather have a fish feast for her wedding than a barbecue, after all.* He was thinking, *Nanny wants me more than she wants a pig or a calf or any fancy meal.* He was thinking, *I want Nan and that is all.* And he thought he might just walk away. For Nanny.

Absalom Johnson knocked Gabriel to the ground; the pig flew for a few good seconds before landing in the road. Too stunned to squeal, the spared swine watched the two men rolling in the dust. Solomon and Jupiter cheered for Gabriel and never remembered that, while a man has his rights, a man's property has none.

Johnson growled into Gabriel's ear, "I saw your bride walkin' alone in the woods. Mighty pretty. Not a mark on her, front or back. Am I right? I need a little gal to cook my meals, wash my clothes. Believe I'll speak to Colonel Wilkinson directly about hirin' her over here."

Gabriel clasped his legs around Johnson's middle and flipped the farmer over onto his back. Sitting on the man's chest, he swore to himself, *Absalom Johnson will suffer for threatening my Nan.* He choked the farmer and wrung his neck until the palette of Johnson's face darkened from apple-blossom pink to overripe persimmon.

I have promised Nanny so much. This fat pig was just the beginning.

Gabriel looked into the farmer's raging green eyes and released his own ferocious rage. He could easily have smashed Johnson's skull against the sharp foot of a rock protruding from the road, and he first thought he might. He heard his brother begging him to stop. So Gabriel grabbed Johnson's shirt and shook him up. "Know this, Absalom Johnson: I am a man with a free will," Gabriel said, and he decided he was about done.

"Oh, I will take her." The defiant farmer snarled his evil intent to harm Nanny.

Gabriel bent down into Johnson's face. "No. From this day, you are a marked man," he said, and imposed on Johnson the common punishment of a desperate master on an insolent slave. With no knife to brand the farmer with, as a slave owner would brand a runaway, Gabriel used his teeth instead. He bit down hard through Johnson's gristly ear until his teeth gnashed against each other and his mouth filled up with warm blood. He clamped his jaw tighter and yanked the ear free.

He removed the farmer's ear for Nanny's protection. With only one ear, Johnson would now be easily identified by any woman the farmer dared approach in the woods or elsewhere. Now the message would be clear to all who saw Johnson: *This man is a danger to our safety.*

Johnson writhed in the dirt. The bleeding man pressed the futile tourniquet of his bare hands against the emptiness on the left side of his head. Blood rushed out, flooding the seams between his fingers, and Johnson kicked at Gabriel, who stood over him.

Jupiter's senses—absent midfight—returned. "What have you done, Gabriel? Lordamercy, what have you done?"

Gabriel wiped his mouth across his bare arm, and,

taking up a handful of red dirt, he rubbed the taste of Absalom Johnson from his mouth.

Solomon took his brother by the elbow. "They'll kill you, Gabriel. Maybe us, too."

Gabriel said to Solomon, "Then 'let justice roll down like water and righteousness like an ever-flowing stream,' Brother."

"What have you done?" Jupiter repeated.

Gabriel put his arm around his good friend. "Come on; we should go."

Unbound and unharmed, the boys set off for Watson's Tavern. They left Absalom Johnson lying in the road. They left the pig to savor the dismembered ear.

Gabriel was hot and flushed from grog when he told Nanny about the fight with Johnson. She popped him good on the head the way she always did when anyone she loved acted a fool. He tried to explain. "I marked him for you, Nan, for your benefit."

When he said *benefit*, Gabriel remembered. *They will not hang me. I will ask for my clergy.*

CHAPTER EIGHTEEN
October 1799

GABRIEL STOOD INSIDE the courthouse along the river in the city exactly one year from Mr. Prosser's untimely passing. He had been in the building many times on business for Jacob Kent, to replace window hinges and door latches. He even had delivered Dr. Foushee's newly shod horse there. This Monday morning, it was where he would answer to charges in the maiming of Absalom Johnson. Maiming was a capital offense for a man like Gabriel.

The court of oyer and terminer—a local tribunal of gentleman justices appointed to try slaves—had earlier dismissed all charges against his brother Solomon, but they hadn't let Jupiter off.

HENRICO COUNTY COURTHOUSE

RICHMOND TOWNE

ON the complaint of Absalom Johnson against SOLOMON, a Negro man, slave, the property of Thomas Henry Prosser of this county, under an apprehension that he, SOLOMON, will destroy him or his property by Fire or other ways. It is the Opinion of the court that the said Complaint be dismissed and the said Negro man, SLAVE SOLOMON, discharged.

In the matter of JUPITER, property of Nathaniel Wilkinson, the court unanimously finds SAID JUPITER guilty of hog stealing. Thirty-nine lashes at the public whipping post near the market house. Guilty. Thirty-nine lashes, well laid on.

Signed
WILLIAM FOUSHEE
HEZEKIAH HENLEY
GERVAS STORRS
GEORGE WILLIAMSON
PLEASANT YOUNGHUSBAND

At Gabriel's trial, Absalom Johnson sat in the front of the court with a scrap-cloth bandage wrapped full around his head. Though a month had passed since the fight, wisps of red and brown and yellow still leaked from the dressing.

He felt the farmer watching him and so met his gaze directly, holding Johnson's eyes to his until the farmer cringed and looked down at his hands. Gabriel turned toward the jurists, all men he had known since childhood, all men who had hired in his services.

"How do you plea?" Mr. Younghusband, the county coroner, asked.

Gabriel listened for the James River. Well past the clearing of throats at the bench and shuffling of papers in the courtroom, just beyond the clopping of horses in the street and creaking of ships at the waterfront, he heard the falls of the James churning and roaring toward the calm, deep port. And in the silent pauses between them all, he heard Ma call him, too.

Where you off to, my strappin' boy? To the market? To the city? My angel-boy, off to the sea?

From a narrow ravine in his heart, Gabriel also heard Pa. *You live free, Gabriel-boy.*

Gabriel stated his plea for the court and every witness present to hear: "Innocent."

The only evidence the court needed was the hollow side of Absalom Johnson's head. They took pity on Johnson, a refugee from the more rural and less refined Dinwiddie County. While the Henrico gentlemen considered their verdict, Johnson burst out that he was afraid of Gabriel. "In Dinwiddie, this villain would have been drawn and quartered already." He begged the court, "He tried to kill me, and he will kill me if you don't take swift and permanent action." The farmer trembled, and his voice cracked.

Gervas Storrs scolded him, "Sir, we all understand you are rather newly arrived to Henrico County. I remind you, we are a genteel and fair-minded people here. I know Prosser's Gabriel, and this could only have been provoked."

"He bit off my ear!" Johnson shouted.

No matter that the gentleman jurists realized that even their own bondmen stole their neighbors' hogs and calves on occasion, no matter that the gentlemen recoiled at the sight of the social-climbing Johnson, and no matter that they themselves had hired Gabriel on—they would punish him severely.

Gabriel's counsel did not show how Johnson had lunged first. His counsel failed to raise the issue of Johnson's foul threat against Nanny. Yet even had the

7 October 1799

HENRICO COUNTY COURTHOUSE

RICHMOND TOWNE

IN the matter of GABRIEL, a Negro man, slave, the property of Thomas Henry Prosser of Henrico, charged with maiming Absalom Johnson of Henrico by biting off a considerable part of his ear, it is the unanimous Opinion of the Court that the SAID GABRIEL is GUILTY. GUILTY of maiming. Hang him by the neck. Hang him at the usual place. Hang him by the neck til he be dead.

Signed
WILLIAM FOUSHEE
HEZEKIAH HENLEY
GERVAS STORRS
GEORGE WILLIAMSON
PLEASANT YOUNGHUSBAND

defense presented all that and more, the five Henrico gentlemen of the court of oyer and terminer would have returned the same exact verdict.

Gabriel leaned over to his adviser and spoke the three words that he knew would save him: "Benefit of clergy."

"What?" The man representing Gabriel had already begun packing up.

"Request my clergy. It is my right."

Any slave found guilty of a capital crime—save insurrection—could save himself from death by reciting for the court a verse from the Bible. Every man in the room knew the law. Instead of hanging, the guilty man would be branded with a cross in the web of his left hand so that he could never again invoke the stay.

Absalom Johnson rose to his feet and shook his fist at the court in protest.

"He will be allowed his clergy," said Pleasant Younghusband. "If Prosser's Gabriel can stand before us and recite a verse from memory, we will stay this execution. Jailer? Ready the brand."

Gabriel rose before the court. He thought of Ma and the psalms she had taught him under the apple tree when he was a boy. He recalled Ma's lost love of the scripture and how she believed, even in the first days after Pa had been taken, that her Lord was on the side of freedom. He wished Ma had been right.

He made his selection and spoke the verse in full voice. He glared at Johnson and recited, " 'Such people dig a deep hole, then fall in it themselves. The trouble they cause comes back on them, and their heads are crushed by their own evil deeds. Psalm seven, verses fifteen and sixteen.' "

Absalom Johnson dropped his head in his hands and wept openly before the court. His weeping quickly turned to wailing.

Gabriel did not wince when the jailer pressed the bright-orange cross into his hand. He didn't turn away at the smell of his own singed flesh but only wondered whether he had actually forged this very brand the last time he hired out to Gervas Storrs.

Unanimously, the tribunal disapproved of the way Thomas Henry Prosser allowed Gabriel to move about the countryside unchecked and even into the city, though every man on the court had made use of Gabriel's services for his own personal gain.

When Mrs. Younghusband desired an entry gate to her garden—one adorned with forged rosettes— Pleasant Younghusband had hired on Gabriel. No other blacksmith possessed the skill or patience to meet Mrs. Younghusband's standards of quality. The coroner detested the practice of hiring out, which allowed bondmen to earn cash. "It undermines our entire system," he often said, but his wife's contentment mattered most.

What bothered William Foushee was Gabriel's pride. "If only he would act more agreeable, more aware of a man's stature," Foushee said. "Why, he even refuses to call Prosser himself 'master.'"

"Agreed, Dr. Foushee. He swaggers about the city and the countryside with the airs of a man born of a higher position," Gervas Storrs observed.

Nor did the court hold Thomas Henry guiltless of Gabriel's conduct. "Had young Prosser maintained proper control over his property," Hezekiah Henley reasoned, "Johnson would have his ear, the pig his slop, and we would all be melting butter over our Sally Lunn bread."

"They both love money above all else. Let them each feel this in the deepest possible way," George Williamson recommended.

The gentlemen of the court of oyer and terminer sentenced Gabriel to jail and set his bail at one thousand dollars. The upstart planter and his proud bondman could reckon with each other over who would pay. With further punishment and high bond set, the court sent this message to Thomas Henry Prosser: *Get control of your property!*

Thomas Henry may have desired wealth above all else, but the court was mistaken about Gabriel. He desired something other than money. Whosoever believed a hot brand, a jail term, and a high bond would sour Gabriel on liberty would soon discover that Gabriel was, indeed, born of a higher mind than the court had reckoned.

CHAPTER NINETEEN
November 1799

HE HOPED Nan would wait. He hoped that when he returned, she would still marry him, as they had planned. For the month Gabriel sat in the damp, sour jail with no word from Thomas Henry and no way to get word to Nanny, this hope saw him through each day. *I'll return to Brookfield, and I will marry Nanny.*

For the first week of his sentence, he kept near the door of his cell, looking out, sure his old playmate would come. At two weeks, he let himself recline against the crumbling clay wall, still certain: *Thomas Henry will come.*

At three weeks, Gabriel would have cursed himself for having had any faith in anyone, but every day

Jacob Kent passed fish and greens and hard biscuits through the outer cell window. Gabriel's teacher also brought news from the smithy—a source of sustenance. "The whole city is talking about you. Some are cautious. Worried about what might be brewing in the hearts of bondmen. Others say you are a hero. All agree you are a man to be feared," Jacob told him.

"No reason for anyone to be afraid as long as I sit in this cell. Thomas Henry should be scared to his core for when I get out." He didn't bother to lower his voice.

Gabriel ate every bit of the food Jacob brought him and spared no morsel for the rats that shared his cell. For them, he left the watery porridge provided once daily by the jailer.

In early November, Thomas Henry finally appeared at the jail. "Come with me now. I have been summoned to court to guarantee your good behavior, including and especially toward Absalom Johnson," he said to Gabriel.

Without glancing up from his spot by the cell door, Gabriel asked, "How can one man guarantee the acts of another?"

Thomas Henry ground his teeth together. "I know you better than anyone. Come with me now."

"No. I know *you*. You are the same boy, lit with

greed yet still not King Carter." He would wait in jail forever before he groveled to Thomas Henry.

Thomas Henry pursed his lips and stiffened his jaw. "Gabriel, you're coming home, and I must sacrifice a great deal for your release. It will cost me a thousand dollars to get you out of here and will cost you the same. The question is, how will you repay me?"

Gabriel turned toward the window, away from the cell door, away from Thomas Henry.

"We were friends once," Thomas Henry said.

"I was a child," Gabriel replied. He stroked the place on his forehead that marked the day Thomas Henry became a man. "You have grown up more barbaric than your father."

"Gabriel, your father was a rascal, to be sure, but I don't recall him gnawing off a man's ear." Thomas Henry lowered his voice so that only Gabriel could hear him. "I can tolerate your night walking to the colonel's place, your impending marriage, which will yield me nothing, and even your sauntering here, there, and yon as you please. But this . . . this business with Johnson." Thomas Henry's temple swelled up and throbbed out in time with his heart. The young planter pressed his forehead against the bars. His voice cracked. "My peers whisper behind my back. My future father-in-law reprimanded me in public. The gentle-men of the court—my father's friends—" Thomas Henry stopped talking when the jailer passed by.

Sometimes when Gabriel listened out the cell win-dow, he heard the people talking nonsense—the boat-men, the washerwomen, the laborers of Richmond. Yet sometimes they spoke of a faraway island, convinced their freedom would soon come. And sometimes in the mornings, he heard them sing of Gabriel and glory and righteous peals of thunder. He needed out.

Gabriel turned back over and said to Thomas Henry, "I got five hundred hidden away. I can get you your money only if you get me out." He stood up, and the usually unflappable rodents scattered away under the bed and back into the walls.

After the court released them, Thomas Henry sat ready to drive back to Brookfield in the same cart that had brought Gabriel to Richmond when he was a boy. The leather seat was now torn, its stuffing falling out, and the bay mare's muzzle was turning white.

Gabriel bypassed Thomas Henry and headed east down Main Street, toward Jacob Kent's forge, in the opposite direction from Brookfield.

The Prosser cart pulled up beside him. "Stop! Gabriel, get in here right now!" Thomas Henry

HENRICO COUNTY COURTHOUSE

RICHMOND TOWNE

THOMAS Henry Prosser appeared here in open Court and produced GABRIEL, a Negro man, slave, the property of the said Prosser. It is ordered that the said Thomas Henry Prosser be bound to find security for the good behaviour of the SAID GABRIEL and his keeping the peace towards all the good people of this Commonwealth for the space of twelve months from this time.

Signed
GEORGE WILLIAMSON
PLEASANT YOUNGHUSBAND

shouted while he fought to bring Old Major's bay mare to a halt. "Your pride and your insolence have cost you an awful lot lately."

Gabriel kept walking.

"Do you want to end up back in jail?" Thomas Henry stood shouting in the gig.

He kept walking.

"Are you a common criminal, then?"

People around them stopped minding their business to watch the quarrel unfolding. A constable stepped up to Gabriel's elbow. Still Gabriel kept walking.

"Get in," Thomas Henry ordered.

He refused. "I'll earn you better here in Richmond with Jacob Kent than in Caroline or Hanover. You want your money, you leave me be." Gabriel eyed the constable, who stood ready to assist Thomas Henry, eager to subdue Gabriel. "Leave me be, *Master*."

He did not look back again, even when Thomas Henry called after him, "Wait, Gabriel. We can work this out. Wait."

I have waited too long for too little, Gabriel thought. He neared Jacob's forge and said out loud, to no one but himself, "My plan has changed."

Again, Gabriel took his problem to the fire and the anvil.

CHAPTER TWENTY
November 1799

GABRIEL HAD SEEN Charles Quersey before and shod his stallion, but Jacob had always dealt with the Frenchman directly. This time, Quersey stopped in the smithy to have his pistol repaired and asked for Gabriel.

"I've heard about you," Quersey said. "Are you able to read?" The man handed Gabriel a leaflet telling of America's new alliance with Saint Domingue.

The leaflet was old, from the springtime, yet still Gabriel's spirit was ripe to hear and ready to read how his own liberty was entwined with the now-free Caribbean island.

LETTER
from
A PHILADELPHIA *PATRIOT*
to
ALL *GOOD PEOPLE*
and
FELLOW *PATRIOTS*

❧

by a SINCERE FRIEND *to* FREEDOM

AMERICA STANDS READY to open trade with St. Domingo and the "amiable and respectable" Toussaint L'Ouverture, the BLACK GENERAL! The bill, which even bears the name *Toussaint's Clause,* being recently signed into law by President Adams. After much debate, Adams and Pickering and the Federalists won passage of this bill. Yes! *Toussaint's Clause* should have passed! And with free and open trade, like it or not, comes America's blessing for the island's complete and full independence from France.

———

Now, O Freedom!
Let us look again upon our own shores!

———

Our shores which harbour the true SONS OF LIBERTY. Let us not overlook the thousands of men, women, and children enslaved by the southern states. In fields of cotton and tobacco, on city scaffolds and river bateaus, the Africans work and suffer bondage to fortify and strengthen your young nation.

Will you turn away and leave them suffer alone?

Will you leave them suffer without an Advocate?

Even Daniel of the scripture had help from God above. Yet, has Daniel's God abandoned the Africans? How long until every slave in North Carolina is free? How long before every slave in Virginia experiences the same *joy* and *delight* as Toussaint's soldiers of the French island?

∾ PRINTED IN APRIL 1799 ∾

Gabriel touched the paper to his heart the way Ma used to touch her Bible, then handed the leaflet back to Quersey.

Quersey pressed the page back into Gabriel's hand and also a small card bearing his name. "We are sons of liberty, Mister Gabriel. To truly be American, to be truly French, is to be free. I will not rest until every man is free. And you?" The French visitor left the forge without his gun.

Later, Gabriel asked Jacob, "Do you know Charles Quersey?"

"The Frenchman? Said to have been at Yorktown when 'Wallis surrendered. What's your interest in him?"

Gabriel thought first to fib, but Jacob had never given him reason to run or hide or be anything but a truehearted man. He showed the newsprint to his teacher.

While Jacob read the leaflet, Gabriel watched him and waited for his teacher to look up. "I desire liberty for all the people, too," Gabriel told Jacob. He waited to see, on this day, what kind of patriot Jacob Kent would show himself to be. "Now. Jacob, I want freedom now, not tomorrow or in one year or ten years or one hundred. Right now."

Jacob spoke softly, almost to himself. "You were a

boy when you came here, wearing those damned fancy clothes that belonged to someone else and those small shoes that pinched up your feet. Not the casings of a smithy, eh? No, you were not yet the strapping, gifted smith standing here. But on the afternoon when we first met, I knew who you were." He touched Gabriel's temple. "You are your father's son, Gabriel. Privileged men's notions of a convenient liberty could never fool you or your father. And, Just-Gabriel, you are a man now." Holding the paper, Jacob's hands trembled. "Will you agree that your old teacher has treated you fairly?"

Gabriel took the aged, familiar face in his hands. *I could never hurt you, Jacob,* Gabriel thought, then he tried to explain. "Teacher, I was going to marry Nan. I planned to buy her freedom and then mine, but Johnson threatened to harm her. There is no law to protect my woman from such a villain. I am a man, Jacob. Nanny's man. What was I supposed to do?" Gabriel asked. "What am I supposed to do right now?"

Jacob nodded slowly. "Son, there is no *right now* with liberty. Freedom takes time and patience."

"I have never disagreed with you, but, truth is, there is only *right now*. And there is only one choice left for this business of liberty," Gabriel told him.

"Do not mistake politics for principles. Adams is on Toussaint's side because of America's concerns with France, not because America believes in Toussaint," said Jacob.

"Jacob, is freedom not America's concern?" Gabriel asked him. "This forge is your own. You work and move about the city as you please. Do you love your freedom?"

"None but the wealthiest men among us move about fully as they please," said Jacob.

Gabriel lowered his head in disappointment.

"You deserve your freedom because you are entitled from birth," the old smith continued. "Liberty is a God-given right, Gabriel, not for man to dispense or withhold at will. But, son, I am old now. I have lived through one war."

"But this is the unfinished business of your war," said Gabriel. "There is no other choice left for me. Will you help me?"

The old man clung to Gabriel. "Yes, I will always be here, should you need me."

For six weeks, Gabriel worked in Jacob's forge, before returning to Brookfield. Jacob gave Gabriel the larger share of his profits for that time, and soon the Henrico blacksmith's pocket was full of money.

Still, the money he had earned was not enough to fully repay the bond to Thomas Henry and not nearly enough to manumit Nanny.

I return with only my heart and my hands to offer her, Gabriel thought, and he walked on back to Henrico.

Over and over on the road, he stopped, unfolded Quersey's leaflet, and looked at the written-down story of Toussaint L'Ouverture's success. He opened up the page to see the truth: all the world over, humanity now reached up to God and people reached out to each other for freedom.

Alone on the way back to Nanny, Gabriel recalled Toussaint's cry to his people: "Death or liberty!"

Toussaint raised an army of four thousand and repelled the French and the British troops. Toussaint, who can read and write. Toussaint, but a slave. Toussaint, the black general. He thought of the game he and Thomas Henry once played.

"Yes!" Gabriel said aloud. "Death or liberty!" This time, the words were not a game to him, for now Gabriel believed.

CHAPTER TWENTY-ONE
December 1799

WHEN GABRIEL RETURNED to Henrico, the harvest was all picked and winter nearly arrived. The tobacco at Young's and at Brookfield was being pressed into the hogsheads, good separated from bad, and readied for the market. An early snow had come and gone already. Trace mounds of white clung to the shady hollows around the brook, but as was often wont to occur in a Virginia December, the sun interrupted the dead season to mimic springtime for a day or two.

So on Saturday afternoon, Gabriel went to meet the folks under the apple tree at Brookfield. They would make their way to Brook Bridge to meet up with the kin of blood and the kin of spirit—kin from all around the neighboring farms. Such a warm winter

Saturday stirred people from all around the country-side. The time permitted them to leave their work was short, so all the people made haste to Young's spring.

Once gathered, the little children would go and sneak their feet into the ice-cold creek. The elders would be there, counting among themselves who still lived and lamenting together what they had been left to endure. Yet, despite the burdens laden on each, on this day, the people would make praise.

Gabriel reached the meeting place by his tree early. He could hardly keep up with the anxieties swirling through his mind. *Will Nanny want me? What if she fell in love with Jupiter while I was in Richmond? What if the old colonel sold her south? Or hired her out to Johnson?*

Gabriel took the pamphlet from Charles Quersey out of his pocket. He sat beneath the apple tree, reading, awash in the liberation of Saint Domingue. For a time, he set his own yoke down. President Adams's recognition of Toussaint's leadership swelled a new kind of belief in Gabriel—the kind of hope for himself and his kin that could not be bought, even with all the money he might make for the rest of his life.

They broke free! Liberty prevails on Saint Domingue. A man like me—Toussaint! Toussaint saved his people with a heart and a sword for freedom, and now America protects Toussaint! Ma would invoke the Lord God if she were here with me, Gabriel thought. For the first time in his twenty-three years, Gabriel now asked something of God, too.

If you be the true God, Gabriel prayed, *then tell me, who will save me and my people?*

It was Nanny's voice, not God's, that answered. His beautiful woman came running up the hill, waving her arms and calling his name. "Gabriel! Gabriel, it's you!"

Solomon and Martin could not keep up with her, and Jupiter could not keep up with any of them. Nanny slid under Gabriel's shoulder. "It's you they're askin' for at the spring; we've been lookin' all over for you. Come, join us!" Nanny took up his hand and kissed the mark of the cross, only recently seared into his palm. "Come! We're all waitin' for you."

Wearing her best dress, one she had made herself from the handed-down wedding gifts of sky-blue cotton fabric and yellowing old lace, Nanny hooked her arm through his and led him down the hill. "We are way late jumpin' the broom. I waited for you, Gabriel. We all waited for you; no more waitin' now."

He let Nanny pull him down the hill a few steps, then he stopped her. "Toussaint won, Nan." He held the worn article out to her. "Have you heard?"

Nanny covered up Gabriel's hand with hers. "Come to my house tonight as my husband and read this story to me by the fire."

They had no hog, no calf or great feast of any kind. Gabriel did not even have time to run get his own handed-down gift of Jacob's old velvet overcoat. In his soiled, graying work shirt, he married Nanny by the creek on a May Saturday in December, so common to Virginia.

He returned to the countryside with a cross burned into his hand and having barely escaped the gallows. He had relinquished all of Nanny's freedom money and more to Thomas Henry and so had no wedding gift to offer. No way to keep his promise. Yet by the time he married her, Gabriel could see the only true way. Now his true purpose no longer lay dormant or hidden within. *The way* was clear now. The work of his life was not to make fire but to make freedom. After the wedding, Nanny received the congratulations of the women, and Gabriel gathered the men near to talk about the business of liberty.

CHAPTER TWENTY-TWO
December 1799

HE'S MY HUSBAND NOW, Nanny said to herself. She kissed Gabriel's hands while he slept.

How I have missed these hands.

On their wedding night, Nanny made it so that Gabriel rested well. While Gabriel slept, she sat curled up on the bed with her knees tucked around his shoulders. She laughed at how his feet hung well off her bed and smiled at how he had not complained but instead promised to build them a new bed—one with room enough for a man and his wife to love each other good.

Nanny kissed his eyes. *How I have missed this man.*

She cradled his head against her thighs, and with her finger, she drew along the two scars on his forehead, and then she kissed those places. "Here, too, they marked you. I know this story."

She traced Gabriel's long and bony, lovely brown face until all his twitching ceased. She touched the two scars again, then lingered her fingers over his brow. She followed the outline of Gabriel's nose, his chin, and by the time she reached his lips, Gabriel was deep in sleep. She watched him until his eyes darted back and forth under his lids.

Nanny's mind was too busy for sleep, so she rose to sew and clean by the moonlight.

Tomorrow is Sunday, a day of rest even for the likes of me. I'll sleep tomorrow, under the tree, and make Gabriel let me set my head in his lap to catch up on these lost hours.

She could tell Gabriel hadn't washed in weeks; his britches smelled of red cedar and apple wood, smoke, and hard work. She picked up his shirt and pants from the floor, and while he slumbered, Nanny beat his clothes free of all flecks and bark and briars.

He is my husband now. I will care for him, she resolved. She could, at least, sew a new shirt for him, so when one got too soiled, he could wear the other.

When Nanny finally grew tired, she crawled beneath the quilt she had long ago pieced with her sisters, the only remnant of her family. She put her head on Gabriel's chest. Anchored to the rhythm of her husband's breath, Nanny had just slipped into the dreamy cove when Gabriel's fit woke her. Thrashing and kicking, he called out in words she could not understand. The firelight glowed amber across Gabriel's face.

Even in his sleep, Nanny thought, *he finds no peace.*

She tried to cast off the nightmare. "You're safe with me," she whispered to him.

When he cried out, "Water! Water!" Nanny sprang from the bed. She dipped her cup in the wooden bucket and held the water to Gabriel's lips. His eyes shot open, yet he slept on in the grip of the night terror.

Nanny shook him. "Here, drink. You asked for water."

He pushed her hand away. "No. I'm meeting him," Gabriel said.

"Who?" she asked, and tried again to shake him awake. "Who, Gabriel?"

"I'm meeting him at the water," he repeated. "About the business." He fell back on the bed, and Nanny lay awake, watching over him.

In the morning, when she heard Gabriel stir, she first-thing said to him, "Tell me about the business. Who you plan on meeting at the water, Gabriel?"

He revealed how the Frenchman had sought him out at Jacob's forge. He read Nanny the pamphlet. "Can I not do for Virginia what Toussaint has done for his people?" he asked her.

At first after he told her, Nanny wanted Gabriel's plan to be from God. "Has the Lord shown you the way? Did you have a vision?" she asked him.

"I think I have always had this vision, Nan. Is my plan of God? I can only hope."

"Do you hear voices, Gabriel, tellin' you what to do? Where to go? What to say?"

"I have heard these voices since I was a little boy—Ma's, Pa's, Old Major's. Yours, my own, those of the children we will have."

"And you can imagine not only a free Nanny or free Gabriel but a free Virginia?"

"The entire world is turning free. Since childhood, I have asked myself, 'Why not my home?' A free Virginia is all I can imagine."

Nan let her eyes wander the room, searching for some answer, some insight into what to say or do next. She knew she had married a truehearted man, but Nanny had not expected sorrow—the frequent companion of truth—to interrupt her nuptials like this. Seeing no way to change her husband and not sure she wanted to, she implored her Lord God to set aside the quiet and steady work He was known to love in favor of a glorious, bold, and victorious swift Hand. She gave her own hands over to Gabriel. "I am your wife," Nanny said. "I will never abandon you, not even in death. What will we do?"

And Gabriel told Nanny of his plan.

"We will raise an army from the city, from the countryside, and from the waterfront. We will arm our soldiers with swords forged from pitchforks and scythes. We will field a cavalry of borrowed stallions and raid Mr. Jefferson's capitol. We will do whatever it takes, Nan, whatever it takes."

CHAPTER TWENTY-THREE
Spring 1800

COMMONWEALTH *of* VIRGINIA
EXECUTIVE COMMUNICATIONS, 1800
to JAMES MONROE, GOVERNOR

March 23
Arsenal

Sir, this Certifies to the delivery in good order
by Captain John Tinsley of five hundred and
twenty-six cartridge boxes, made by him
according to contract and deposited in the
Arsenal.

May 30
Arsenal

Excellency, the cleaning and stamping of the
arms is progressing well. The muskets are
stamped with the name of the county and
number of the regiment.

June 14
Richmond

Sir, influenced by the idea which generally
prevails, that some precautions are necessary
at the present period in consequence of the
disbanding of the troops in the vicinity of
this place, permit me to invite the attention
of Your Excellency to the propriety of
establishing a guard at the Capitol for a short
period.

———

HE KNEW now was the time to act. After months of private talks and clandestine conversations with Quersey at taverns and in shops around the city—in Jacob's forge, too—Gabriel was ready to recruit men from the city and the countryside.

Governor Monroe had discharged the regiments back home, so the capital lay largely unguarded. All the arms of the militia had been cleaned and tagged and deposited at sites throughout the region. New shipments of gunpowder and bullets were arriving in Richmond from Philadelphia.

On a night when Thomas Henry had long left for the mountains in Amherst County to visit family, Gabriel called the first meeting of the men closest to him. He waited at the smithy to see who among his friends would keep his word. Who among them loved liberty. Who among them was true.

Sitting on a log outside the shop, he let the dark woods fill him with words and resolve. Even more than any man or woman, the oak and the elm and the walnut had long witnessed the oppression of folks in Virginia. These trees attended his people's suffering, anointed their spirits. Now Gabriel asked the forest and his ancestors to breathe wisdom and courage into him. Pa, Old Major, Ma. His stillborn brother.

Grandmothers and grandfathers he had never known. He reached into the past and into the future; he needed all of his people now.

Just before the appointed hour and from every direction, the night beamed, alight with the glow of pine-knot torches ascending the hill, converging on the forge. Old men of proven genius and young men of tested strength united to dream of their freedom and to take their place, a free people.

Thomas Henry's deceitful dealings with Gabriel of late had turned every Henrico bondman against the young planter, though at first some of the elders had blamed Gabriel—not for stealing the hog but for assaulting Absalom Johnson.

All the folks had felt repercussions from that act. Planters in Henrico were like chickens in a henhouse—reacting to every squawk of every nearby neighbor. Some elders said in private and a rare few to Gabriel's face, "Gabriel got a chance. He came close, but he threw his chance away." Yet when Gabriel explained to them in his own words the act of maiming Johnson, all of the gathered men acknowledged the impossibility of restraint. All agreed they could bear no more.

"Then gather close and listen. Now is the time to

rise and fight for our freedom. I have a plan for our liberty. You know me. I'm asking you to stand up."

Gabriel told his early recruits the story of Toussaint, and though they knew of Saint Domingue's victory already, Gabriel gave the story new meaning for these Virginia men.

"Do you think you are too small to make a difference? Tell me, who could imagine this: our brother, Toussaint, showing the world how each man is his own master? Who could imagine a slave boy growing up to command an army? Who could ever dream up a nation of slaves uniting to break free from the irons the whole world conspired to keep them in? Together, are we too small to make a difference?"

The men kept still, and Gabriel gave them the time they needed to place themselves in Toussaint's skin. Gabriel burned a kindling fire that gave off just enough dim light, just enough, to judge each man's face.

He watched how they breathed, and when the rapid, shallow breaths of men shackled by fear subsided, and when Gabriel could see the tide of their bellies rising and falling, he spoke again. "You can imagine this, can't you? You have always held this vision of liberty there inside you, for your whole life.

At first it feels dangerous to return to the free place, the free place where your true spirit lives. At first you might feel wrong. I fooled myself, too. But can we ever be happy without also being free? Can we ever be who God intended us to be? Freedom is ours by God as much as it is Prosser's or Young's or Wilkinson's."

He waved a letter of support and promise of training and troops and arms from Charles Quersey. Most of the recruits had always relied on Gabriel to help them read important documents, but for those who could read, Gabriel made show of handing over every letter of support and offer of assistance. His friend Sam Byrd nodded after reading the letters himself.

"I am a free man; you are free men. Do you believe me?" Gabriel asked them. "We have every right to fight for our freedom as did Washington and Monroe. Now is the time to fight. Will you join me?"

Two brothers stepped forward. "You have our hands and our hearts," they pledged. "We will sooner wade to our knees in blood than give up the fight."

One by one they enrolled. Some of Brookfield's men were among the early joiners—Solomon, Martin, Ben, Tom, Watt, Frank, and Peter. And, from old Colonel Wilkinson's place, Gabriel's good friend Jupiter and also Sam and Nat stepped up. From nearby Mr. Burton's, the husband of Venus, Isaac, and the brothers Isham and George. And from the widow's came the boy Michael. Only Sheppard's Pharoah did not step up.

Gabriel wrote each name on a paper he carried with him. If a man could write, that man signed his name. Those who could not write were required to take up the pen and dip it in the inkwell, which Gabriel kept at the forge. Each one made a bold mark where Gabriel pointed.

He told Michael, "Here is your name, right below *Isaac.*"

The slave Michael looked at the letters in his name. "When I get to be a free man, I will learn to read and write."

"Are you a true man?" Gabriel asked him.

Michael nodded.

"Mark it here."

Throughout the spring of 1800, Gabriel and Solomon and Jupiter persuaded men from all around to enlist with the rebellion. In quiet corners of nearby taverns and on the fringes of public gatherings of folks from nearby quarters—gatherings where the women ate all the fish and the men drank only grog—the liberty boys went about building the liberty business.

CHAPTER TWENTY-FOUR
Summer 1800

GABRIEL CONVINCED men from Caroline and Hanover and Henrico to join the boys on the brook, and many new ones from Richmond came in, too. The boatmen heard talk upriver to Cartersville and down into Petersburg, and more names and more men joined Gabriel's clandestine plan. In Norfolk, in Gloucester, Albemarle, and Dinwiddie, bondmen pledged to fight for their country.

The boys promised guns, clubs, knives, and sticks. They committed to getting horses when the time came to fight. Solomon laid claim to Brookfield's bay mare, Gabriel to Thomas Henry's gray stallion. When the new soldiers asked for details of the plot, Gabriel demurred. "We will train with the French colonel.

For now, gather weapons or bring me your tools," Gabriel said.

Recruits brought scythes for Gabriel and Solomon to repurpose into swords. They turned over pistols for the two blacksmiths to repair.

Wherever men congregated, Gabriel went there to make fire with their true spirits and truest desires. At Half Sink, Littlepage, Hanover Towne, and Ground Squirrel, every boy fell in behind him, clamoring for Gabriel's favor; each boy held his hand out to receive the blacksmith's touch. Now no man dared whisper behind Gabriel's back. Now not even the elders would anymore mention the name Absalom Johnson. Gabriel looked deep into the faces of the boys and men who came to him. He gazed into their true spirits as if they had always been free, as if all of them had always been free.

"Can you keep a secret?" he asked the boys at Half Sink.

"We are about to rise and fight for our freedom," he whispered beneath the bridge at Littlepage.

"I'm damned glad to hear it!" Frank said.

"Can you be strong?" asked Gabriel.

Frank leaped to his feet, ready to fight. Willing to die.

"Then take the oath; swear to secrecy," Gabriel insisted.

And Frank swore, "I am bound not to discover our secret to man, woman, or child or any person who has not genius or strength enough to support us. I will stand by you till the last."

Man after man stood up to take the oath to fight for freedom. In secret, Gabriel and the boys readied the city and countryside for war. Hundreds, and soon thousands, joined with the business.

CHAPTER TWENTY-FIVE
August 1800

COMMONWEALTH *of* VIRGINIA
EXECUTIVE COMMUNICATIONS, 1800
to JAMES MONROE, GOVERNOR

August 9
Mr. Grammer to Mr. Davis
Petersburg

Sir, Some whispers have been heard here
within a few nights past indicating some plan
of an insurrection among the blacks, it is said,
intended to-night or some Saturday night.
The evidence is not sufficient for any steps
to be taken publicly, nor is it publicly known
here. It is, perhaps, prudent that the citizens
should be on their guard and take such steps as

may most likely lead to a detection, if such a thing should be really in agitation. Also, please procure from Mr. Collins, and send me by the stage on Monday or Tuesday, 4 oz. Norfolk Turnips, 2 oz. Hanover Turnips.

August 10
Dr. McClurg to the Governor
Richmond

Dear Sir, This intelligence was received by Mr. Davis in a letter from the Postmaster at Petersburg, and communicated last night by Mr. Davis to me. It appeared to be vague and uncertain; stated that there were whispers of an intended insurrection among the Negroes at Petersburg, and that the information was intended to put the citizens of Richmond upon their guard, as the scheme might extend to this place. At that time of night I thought it best to apply to Capt. Austing, of the Horse, and Lieut. Dunmore, of the Light Infantry, and request that they would form a patrol for the night.

——

GABRIEL FELT a sort of restlessness among his men. One Sunday, with all the people gathered at the brook for a sermon—as their masters commonly encouraged them to convene for worship—he slipped out of the crowd and retreated to below the bridge. The boys involved in the business joined him there and overwhelmed him with questions.

"When will we march?"

"How many men are committed? What about weapons?"

"Why don't we start?"

Ben, one of Brookfield's men, confronted Gabriel. "Why should we put our trust in you? How many names are on your list? How well armed are we?"

Every other man averted his eyes, and this told Gabriel something. *If they are too cowardly to confront me, how will they find the courage to march?*

Gabriel tried to quell their fears. "Solomon and I have made twelve dozen swords. I've made five hundred bullets. Men are bringing what they can bring."

"Those swords will never be enough to take Richmond," Ben said.

Then Sam Byrd reported, "I got five hundred on my list. I'll have every man in Petersburg before long."

Ben would not be satisfied with their answers.

"Gabriel, how many names? Are you marching us to our certain deaths?"

A grumbling spread through them. One or two recruits started back toward the women.

I'm losing them, Gabriel thought. *If Ben goes, they may all go.* "How many will join us? One thousand in Richmond, six hundred from Ground Squirrel Bridge, four hundred in Goochland." He pleaded for help from the sky. "I have ten thousand names! Read for yourself. Count them; read each name aloud for all of us to hear." Gabriel thrust his papers to Ben, who he knew could not read.

When Ben handed the list of names back to him, Gabriel reassured all of the men. "We are strong enough to get the business done."

"How will you make enough arms to take Richmond?" the late recruit Sheppard's Pharoah then asked.

"No need. If you were paying close watch the way I do, you'd know we need only enough force to take Goodall's Tavern. The militia deposited arms there for counting and repair." He heard the grumbling begin to shift back his way.

"My brother's right," Martin said. "The governor ordered the militia to disarm. We can arm ourselves easily at Goodall's and from there march to the capitol."

Gabriel spoke again. "I sent Jupiter to Bob Cooley, who guards all the buildings at the capitol. Mister Cooley has agreed to leave the armory unlocked. We need only say when." This was enough to rouse the boys into full swing and secure their confidence in Gabriel.

Gabriel told them no more. Some were content to know that he had a plan and that French officers stood on their side and at the ready. For others, Gabriel's decision to send Sam Byrd to enlist the Catawba Indians and the poor whites and the free blacks stoked their spirits.

"When they see we are black and white and Indian, our victory will be assured. Death or liberty, boys!" they shouted.

Ben persisted in his doubts and called for the men to vote on who should lead the business, and by a large margin, the boys on the brook elected Gabriel their general.

"Why are we waiting? Let us move the business forward now!" cried Gilbert. "General Gabriel, lead us to the capital city tonight!"

Disagreement rose up among them about when to

move ahead with the business. George said he needed more time. He had recruited only fifty men from Manchester and thirty-seven from Hungry meeting-house. "Defer the business for as long as possible. We need every man," George argued.

"Summer's about over. We must avoid fighting a winter war," Gilbert countered.

After worship at Young's spring, while the women cooled their ankles in the brook and while sisters and friends rejoiced in the company of one another, the men took a second vote — this time to determine the date of the insurrection. The boys defied the permits burning in their pockets and voted that the business of liberty would move forward the next Saturday night, August 30, 1800.

CHAPTER TWENTY-SIX
August 30, 1800

GABRIEL WAS TO MEET Solomon and Jupiter in the forest at his shop on the morning of the appointed Saturday for final preparations. The two brothers reached the shop at the same time. Gabriel made fire; he would cast more bullets and cut more swords while they waited for Jupiter and for nightfall.

Gabriel expected four hundred, five hundred, maybe one thousand men from Goochland, Henrico, Hanover, and Caroline. Another thousand armed soldiers would fall in with them at Richmond. The rest would join once they took the city. He had ordered them to meet at Brook Bridge; all were to bring what arms they could secure. Some would bring clubs and sticks; others would carry the weapons that Gabriel and Solomon had crafted from the scythes used to cut tobacco and wheat. A few would take swords off great-house mantels and rifles from under great-house beds. They would gather at midnight, and he would need every hour until then to make ready.

Will these last bullets give us victory? he asked himself.

"If we use the coming night to fight. If we remember we are men with an equal right to freedom," Gabriel said, not realizing he spoke out loud.

"What, Brother?"

"We've done all we can do," he told Solomon. "Our deliverance is in our hands." To himself, he prayed for God to be real and on the good side of the business.

All morning, the brothers worked alone and in quiet, readying the small, homemade arsenal to move to Brook Bridge once the sun set. Just past noon, Gabriel heard Nanny calling him. She had run all the way from Wilkinson's.

"Here," she said, out of breath. "Sit down and eat. Take your nourishment, now. Both of you." Nanny unwrapped two hoecakes and a sweet potato for each brother from her bandanna. "Share this meal with me." Nanny took her husband's left hand and held it tight. "I love you, Gabriel."

He opened Nanny's kerchief and smelled the

still-warm yam, then blew the ashes off. He wiped his hands on his shirt before taking a bite. "I'm wearing my Nanny shirt." He pointed to the delicate red stitches adorning the cuffs near his wrists and lacing the collar at his heart. He told his wife, "Forgive me for not teaching you every word you ever wanted to read."

Nanny shook her head. "You taught me to write our names. And when we are free and eatin' with the merchants of the city, we will take up my lessons again."

In front of Solomon, Gabriel grabbed her around the waist and pulled her in close. "It's a beautiful day for love." But the shop—bustling toward freedom—was too busy for love.

Sam Byrd stopped in to report that the roads looked clear, but to the west the sky did not. Isaac and Ben came to collect their weapons. But Isaac hesitated to take his sword from Gabriel.

"Something wrong with you, Isaac?" Gabriel asked him.

Isaac jutted his chin out. "Nothin' the matter."

"Good. This is a day for men, not chickenhearted boys." Gabriel bumped the young recruit on his way to get more wood for the fire.

Sam Byrd and Ben laughed.

Isaac looked over at Nanny and blurted out, "You

told us not to repeat the business in front of any woman, General."

Gabriel spun around to Isaac, his voice forceful and clear. "Nanny *is* the business; she's not just any woman. We need her. If the business goes bad, and we end up taking to the swamp, she'll run our provisions and messages. Nanny's life will be on the line with ours. What you hear from Nanny, you hear from me. Understand?"

Isaac saluted.

Solomon dunked the bullet mold into a bucket of cool water, and when the burst of steam hissed, Isaac jumped.

"Isaac, it's all right to feel afraid," Nanny said, trying to reassure the unlikeliest of soldiers. Gabriel's eyes met Nanny's. They knew that anyone who backed out now would endanger everyone involved.

"What do I do?" Isaac asked her.

Isaac looks like a child, not a warrior, Gabriel thought. He nodded to his wife that she should answer.

Nanny tried to embolden Isaac. "You will go to Brook Bridge with the sword Gabriel made you. There, one thousand freedom fighters will join you. Your children, wherever they are, will be free because of what you do on this night. Isaac, do you believe me?"

"The business will never work. You know that, don't you, Gabriel?" Ben asked from the corner.

Isaac stood shaking.

Ben didn't hide his doubt. "Our general is sending us to our deaths; the black general is ready to fight. But are you ready to fall, Gabriel? Are you ready to die?"

"Hush your mouth, Ben." Nanny held her hand out to Isaac. "The business will work. Gabriel's army will march into Richmond in three columns. You need only to get to the capitol; there you will re-arm. Bob Cooley will unlock the armory. Some will march to Rocketts and set it on fire to draw the city men away from the capitol. Others will have already taken the weapons from Goodall's Tavern. Another column will take the powder from the penitentiary. All will come back together under Gabriel's command. Once the governor is in our custody, the army will head south to Petersburg, then Norfolk. Along the way, others will join in: Frenchmen, workers, freemen, the Catawba. The business will work. Am I right, Ben?"

Ben stared out the door. "A storm's comin'. Nanny, come see these dark clouds."

Isaac went to the door; Nanny followed and put her arms around his shoulders.

"Ignore him," Nanny said of Ben. "He's not a man today."

Isaac confessed to Nanny, "I don't want to die."

She kissed her friend's forehead. "Shhhh. It's all right; it's all right."

Gabriel threw down his hammer and shouted at Isaac, "Tell me something. Where is Venus? Where did Thomas Henry send her?"

"To Amherst County, across the mountains," Isaac answered.

"Are you sure? Where is your daughter? Your son?"

"Gone. Sold. I don't know why. I don't know where," Isaac answered, staring at the ground.

"Yes, gone. All of them. Aren't you already dying? Look here, what kind of man are you, Isaac?" Gabriel asked. "Your freedom starts in this instant. Right now, you must decide."

Isaac closed his eyes and whispered, "I am a true man."

"I don't believe you."

Isaac cleared his throat. "General Gabriel, here are my hands. Here is my heart. I am ready to fight for my country."

By sunset, the western August sky had darkened, and the rain had arrived. Those first gusts of wind and the early smell of rain did not dissuade them. Gabriel and Solomon and Sam Byrd all agreed that the business would still go forward. They would not turn back. They even believed that the approaching storm might make the work easier to carry out, for it would keep the patrollers inside while the boys took the city.

The storm did not relent. Soon the rain overtook the roads, the creek, and the meadows. The water rose too fast, sweeping cows out of their fields and pulling horses out from under their riders. Heifers and goats scrambled to reach high ground but lost their footing, fell, and drowned by the dozens. Brook Bridge—Gabriel's access to the city—crumbled in minutes. No bridges were left passable because no bridges were left. The places that could once be forded could no longer. Brookfield was cut off from Richmond.

Gabriel waited until his only choice was to postpone the rising until Sunday. He and Jupiter and Solomon and Sam and also Nanny split up to get the word across the countryside: "Abandon the business! We will advance tomorrow instead. Meet at Prosser's tobacco house on Sunday night."

They went from quarter to tavern to quarter, giving the new order to anyone they could find.

CHAPTER TWENTY-SEVEN
August 30, 1800

August 30, 1800
Mosby Sheppard to Governor Monroe
Richmond

Dear Governor,
I have just been informed by two of my hands,
Pharoah and Tom, that the Negroes were to rise (as
they termed it) in the neighborhood of Mr. Thomas H.
Prosser's and to kill the neighbors, viz. Major Wm.
Mosby, Thomas H. Prosser, and Mr. Johnson; from
thence they were to proceed to town, where they would
be joined by the Negroes of this place (Richmond), after
which they were to take possession of the arms and
ammunition, and then take possession of the town.

Here the two stopped, appearing much agitated. I then asked them two questions.

When was it to take place?
Answer: To-night.

Who is the principal man?
Answer: Prosser's Gabriel.

I have given you the substance of what I have heard, and there is no doubt in my mind but what my information is true, and I have given you this information in order that the intended massacre may be prevented if possible.

I am, with due respect,
Mosby Sheppard

N.B. I will here recite to you the manner in which I got this information. I was sitting in the counting-room with the door shut, and no one near except myself; Pharoah and Tom knocked at the door, and I let them in; they shut the door themselves and then began to tell what I have before recited.

CHAPTER TWENTY-EIGHT
August 31, 1800

HE HAD ORDERED his men to stay away on Saturday night. For most of their lives, they had all worked in the rain and mud whenever required, but no one could recall having lived through a storm like this one.

The boys would have braved a rain.

Some did try to reach Brook Bridge. Some drowned in the night. Others stole away to the woods to wait, but even those who escaped the flood would not escape the fate of this day.

By Sunday morning, a day as clean as the night was cruel brought the people out from the quarter to watch the water recede. By Sunday morning, the patrollers knew all about Gabriel's plan. On Sunday morning, a few recruits ran deep into the forest, and a few chose to face the patrollers and fight.

Solomon's voice trembled when he told Gabriel, "They're arresting the boys from Price's, from Mr. Young's. The patrol hunted Michael into the woods. You'd be proud, Brother. He drew his sword, but they were too many. Michael will hang."

Gabriel needed a new plan, yet on this day there was no time to make fire or sound the anvil beat. He knew even more men would soon be overtaken and soon tried and executed.

Solomon looked to his younger brother for reassurance. "Will we all hang, Gabriel?"

"No. Not all of us," Gabriel promised.

Solomon covered his face and wept. Gabriel did nothing but watch Nanny set sweet potatoes in the fire. He looked out at the Sunday-morning sky. The storm had left behind low, luminous, and steep white clouds, seemingly within reach, just there at the canopy. "Almost makes you think we already won. We're looking hard at the bacon, but we can't get to it," Gabriel said.

He watched Nanny turn the potatoes over and nudge them deeper into the heat. When she stretched

her back—low, middling, and high up—he wondered, *How much sleep has she already lost? How many
meals did she skip to save up this food?*

He gathered what weapons he could easily carry—
a pistol and a homemade bayonet. He took bullets,
a scythe-sword, and his papers—the letters from
Quersey, the list of names. Nanny handed him a blan-
ket and a kerchief tied off to hold two days' worth of
food. He didn't have to tell her where he would be or
that he would lie out in the marsh and wait. They both
knew the fate awaiting those men caught at Brookfield
or nearby. Virginia would demand their lives.

"I'll send word to the Frenchman. If I can get to
Norfolk, I'll join our boys there," he told her.

"And Solomon?" Nanny asked.

Gabriel shook his head. "He's not thinking right.
Solomon will stay here."

"I'm comin' with you," Nanny said.

I would give up my own life for the business of liberty,
he thought. *Can I send my own wife to the gallows?*

"Stay here," Gabriel told her. "Be my eyes. Be
my ears. Bring food to me and the men and bring us
news."

He contemplated whether the summer had all

been a great mistake. *How could I ever think any freedom, whether in life or death, would be worth any price if I could not have Nanny?* .

But he knew his campaign was not only about their love. They were fighting for Nanny's sisters, her parents, whom she could not even remember, Venus and Isaac and their children, and Dolly and Joseph, too. He knew Nanny understood all of this.

She raised Gabriel's hand. "Death or liberty! I'll find out what I can and then come find you in the swamp."

A delicate trace of regret constricted around his heart. Gabriel held his wife close and admitted, "The boys call me General Gabriel. I'm scared, Nan."

"I know." Nanny kissed his left palm, his hammer hand, so much larger than the other. "I won't ever leave you." Then she brought his hand to her stomach. "I know for sure our child is growing here," Nanny said.

Gabriel sank to his knees and pressed his face to Nan's dress. *How can I leave Nan?*

Yet, even knowing Nanny was carrying their child, Gabriel did not change his course. All along, he had been fighting for Nanny and for the son or daughter whose reflection they first saw in the creek. Certain his child was protected in the darkest, safest place of all and sure that remaining at Brookfield would mean certain condemnation to the gallows, Gabriel mustered all his courage to forge on with the business.

Nanny stirred the embers of his belief. "You are my Toussaint, our black general. You are my Gabriel, our freedom fighter." She pressed the sack into his hands, though these supplies would not last long in the marsh. "I promise your son will know. Your son and his daughter and her children will know this: Gabriel did not give up. They *will* know."

"We will see what the day brings," he told her. He told himself, *If I can get to Norfolk, hundreds of soldiers will be waiting, and the Frenchman will be there, too. Our freedom still has a chance.*

Local patrollers descended on Brookfield by horse and by foot. They took Ben and Watt and Peter. They captured Martin and Solomon, too. At Wilkinson's they found Jupiter. And from Burton's place they dragged poor Isaac through the field, down the road, and all the way into the city. But Gabriel escaped to the swamp. The plot had been discovered. Had the business yet failed?

CHAPTER TWENTY-NINE
September 4, 1800

EXECUTIVE COMMUNICATION, COMMONWEALTH *of* VIRGINIA, SEPTEMBER 4, 1800

On further consideration of the conspiracy & Insurrection among the Negroes, it is advised that a party of sixty men be ordered from the militia to patrol for the general safety of the county and particularly about the plantations of Messrs. Wilkinson & Prosser, where it is suggested the conspiracy originated, and that they be instructed to make diligent search for the arms of the conspirators. It is also advised that the Magistrates be permitted to commit witnesses or informers of the plot to the Penitentiary for their security.

GABRIEL SAT in the bough of an old, low oak. His legs rested against a hairy vine that made him itch. Open blisters oozed yellow and green down his arms, but now he hardly noticed. The hoecakes and potatoes Nanny had given him were long ago devoured. He thought he had been awake for days, and with the lapping of the swamp against the oak's great roots, he started to fade. A familiar howl woke Gabriel.

"Ah-oo-oo-oo."

Gabriel leaned against the tree trunk. He wanted to hear the mournful call again. He could not see Dog but heard her moving closer through the water.

"Ah-oo-oo-oo." The hound sounded like she might give up, so desperate her call. To comfort her, Gabriel called back, "Ah-ah-oo-oo." *I'm here, old friend; I'm here.*

"Gabriel?" Nanny appeared beneath the oak in the gleam of the moon.

He dropped from the limb to his wife. Nanny wrapped her arms around Gabriel's neck and burrowed her head into his chest. The news poured out of her. "Patrollers are out along the James, west to Cartersville, and all along the road north to Fredericksburg. Already seven have been hanged at the gallows in Caroline. Some boys were hanged in Hanover, too.

"They took Isaac to Richmond. Tied him to a horse and dragged him away." She could not stop the news from pouring out of her. "Ben, Sam Byrd, Frank, Gilbert, George, poor Jupiter, too—"

"My brothers?"

"Richmond."

Nanny held out a new sack with more food.

Gabriel closed his eyes. *Who will watch over Solomon? He will fall.*

He pulled Nanny's head closer with his chin. "Keep still, Nan. Just like this," he said. *So solid in my arms. Strong enough to live here forever with me in this old swamp,* Gabriel thought. He knew they couldn't return to Brookfield or the colonel's, but they could make a life in the bog.

If she pleads with me to quit the business, I will.

Gabriel wanted only her. More than he wanted his own smith shop or a place to live in town, he wanted to feel Nanny's foot push against his calf every night. He wanted to teach her how to make the letters into even more words and show her how together they could spell any dream a man and wife could imagine. Others had escaped their bondage and lived off the marsh or the forest. For a false minute, Gabriel thought, *We might find our freedom here.*

"I want to make love to my free wife. I want to look into the walnut eyes of our first son and ask him, *Where're you off to, my strappin' boy?*" he said aloud.

In his heart, he heard the words of his older brother Martin, who had said, at the spring, "I have borne all I can bear." He remembered how, when he was a boy, he watched slaves build the city he loved and the capitol itself, where freedom and justice were the business. He looked at his hands that forged such prosperity for Mr. Prosser and Thomas Henry. And he looked at his wife, but a slave who would hang with him if they were ever caught.

Gabriel held his wife close and heaved a great sigh. "Many arrests and, no doubt, more coming. The betrayal begins. What's next?" he asked.

He thought he heard baying dogs and snorting horses, trained to hunt men and game, snaking around the swamp. Shouting and shooting would come next. Whether the arrival of militia was imminent or an audible mirage conjectured by his tired mind, it didn't matter now. The only quiet he heard was the silence from Ma's God, the one who had yet to let His voice be heard or His power be known. Gabriel prayed for a better God.

"I can bear no more," Gabriel finally said to Nanny.

"Then you must go and keep goin'. Find the Frenchman. Sail to Saint Domingue to meet your brother Toussaint and bring back many men," Nanny implored him. She held his hand to her belly. "We are united here—Gabriel and Nanny. Half you and half me."

Gabriel held tight to his wife and their unborn child. The only place he felt true and belonging and free was with Nanny, yet he had not even himself to offer her. His plan to free her had failed; his plan to gain all their liberty was coming undone.

Nanny kissed him. "Remember what you told me?"

"Tell me what."

"You said there's a place inside me that's always been free and will always be. You said there's a place where God lives in me. You said that's where you live, too."

"Yes."

"I believe you," Nanny said.

He shook his head. "My men. The boys will be murdered."

"You delivered them back to the free place, to the untouched, free place. You let each man decide for himself, and they refused to ever forget. Now, what will you do?"

"You know what will happen."

Her tone turned sharp. "No, I don't."

He wavered. "Nan, I will hang."

"If you have no hope, go on and turn yourself in. Die with your men now, before they're all killed. Hang with Solomon and Martin. But if some part of you still believes, if any part of you needs even a single free breath, then you cannot turn back."

Gabriel knew Nanny spoke the truth. He stood in the moonlight wishing he could spirit her away from the days ahead, wishing he could deliver her to a safe place where she could wait for him to come home to her.

"I have to get to Jacob Kent; he can get me to Norfolk," Gabriel said. "First I need to disappear— away from Brookfield, away from the city. If I can get word to you, I will. If you hear nothing more from me, Nanny, you know, I—. You know, don't you?"

"Shhh . . . I will always hear your voice in my heart, in the creek, in these trees." She cradled his head, and when he turned his face to her, she traced his scars, his eyes, his nose, and his lips one last time. "Go. March ahead to Norfolk and bring back an army."

Then Gabriel vanished. He forged no pass and no freedom papers. Would he make Norfolk, find the Frenchman, or, perhaps, reach Saint Domingue?

CHAPTER THIRTY
September 8–9, 1800

September 8, 1800
Magistrates to the Governor
Richmond

Dear Excellency,
This is to certify that we were examining magistrates in the case of the Negroes charged with conspiracy and a design to rebel against the white people; and from every incident which appeared at the examination, we do not hesitate to say that Gabriel, the property of Thomas H. Prosser of Henrico County, was clearly proven to be the main spring and chief mover in the contemplated rebellion.

Given under our hands,
Gervas Storrs
Joseph Selden

A PROCLAMATION

by the GOVERNOR *of the* COMMONWEALTH *of* VIRGINIA

WHEREAS there is good cause to suspect that Gabriel, a Negro slave, the property of Thomas H. Prosser, has been concerned in exciting an insurrection of the Negroes against the Commonwealth, and who hath absconded from justice: I have therefore thought fit with the advice of the Council of State to issue this Proclamation, hereby offering a reward of three hundred dollars to any person who shall apprehend and convey to the jail of the county of Henrico the said Negro slave Gabriel, to the end that he may be tried for the said crime.

And Whereas it is presumable that some of the accomplices of the said Gabriel may have repented of the part they have borne in the said conspiracy and be disposed to make some atonement therefore with a view to confirm them in that disposition, I do hereby in addition to the above reward, to any number not exceeding five of the said accomplices, who shall apprehend the said Gabriel and deliver him up so that he may be brought to justice, offer a full pardon for their said offenses.

All officers civil and military within their respective departments are hereby required, and the good people of the Commonwealth exhorted, to use their best endeavors to apprehend and convey the said Negro slave Gabriel to the jail.

GIVEN under my hand and under the seal of the COMMONWEALTH at RICHMOND, this 9th day of SEPTEMBER, ONE THOUSAND EIGHT HUNDRED.

JAMES MONROE

N.B. Gabriel is a Negro of a brown complexion, about six feet, three or four inches high, a bony face, well made, and very active, has two or three scars on his head, his hair is very short, and has lost two front teeth.

He can read and write and perhaps will forge himself a pass, or certificate of his freedom. He is about twenty-four or twenty-five years of age but appears to be about thirty.

CHAPTER THIRTY-ONE
September 11, 1800

THE TRIAL OF SOLOMON,
11 SEPTEMBER 1800
Evidence against Solomon,
the property of Thomas Henry Prosser

WITNESS, PROSSER'S BEN:

"*Solomon made swords to carry out the plan, Gabriel's plan. Solomon was the Treasurer. First, they planned to kill Mr. Prosser and Mr. Johnson, then all the White neighbors. The plan was for the Saturday night with such a great fall of rain. Their meeting place was near Prosser's Blacksmith shop in the woods. After attacking our neighborhood, they planned to march ahead to Richmond to take the Arms and Ammunition. Gabriel was to command them from the very start of the business. The swords made by Solomon was for Gabriel to give to his men. They had been making those swords ever since last Harvest. One thousand men was to be raised from*

Richmond, six hundred from Ground Squirrel Bridge, and four hundred from Goochland. They would meet at William Young's, whenever the people gathered for a preachment or Fish feast or a Barbecue. They would meet to plan the Insurrection. That big Rain what fell on Saturday night stopped them. Solomon made the swords what was to be used by their Horse Men. They already had two hundred but said there would be four hundred Horse Men. Gabriel & Solomon kept lists of the names of the men. I saw the names. Two white Frenchmen was the first ones to speak of it. I never heard their names."

Witness, Pharoah, the property of Mr. Sheppard: "On that Saturday, Solomon asked me if I saw the light horse of Richmond out. I told him I'd see some at the tavern. Solomon told me the business . . . the plan would go forward even if they got found out. He still had to make more swords, he told me. He told me a thousand men would meet at the Brook."

The court sentences Solomon, a Negro man slave, the property of Thomas Henry Prosser of Henrico, to death on charge of conspiracy and insurrection, and orders that he be hanged by the neck on the twelfth, instant at the usual place of execution.

GABRIEL RODE into Richmond in a cart driven by Tinsley's John. At low twelve on September fourth, he had left the swamp headed north toward Hanover Towne, where he hid out for another week. He had friends, recruits, at the tavern there and prayed they could help him get into the city undiscovered.

Concealed underneath a mound of hay, he hardly breathed the whole twelve miles into town. As the cool September morning broke, the patrollers stopped John and asked for his papers and mulled through the cart, just avoiding the corner where Gabriel had melted away into the wood bottom. He needed to reach Jacob's forge. He knew that to go back into Richmond was dangerous, but he saw no other way to reach Norfolk but down the James.

The boys in Norfolk might be ready to rise. If Quersey went south there, there may be a way.

Gabriel was known to many in the capital and could only hope that if he were to be recognized, it would be by those friends of liberty who had shared Richmond's streets with him since he was an apprentice boy. When he reached Main Street, John drew the cart alongside a quiet alley, and Gabriel slipped away and, with help from the washerwomen, stayed hidden until dusk.

At the forge, Jacob was waiting. They embraced.

"Militia's already come three times to this shop, Gabriel. They'll return; we know that. You go to this spot four miles down the river. Wait there for the schooner called *Mary;* go see Captain Richard Taylor. He'll get you to Norfolk. Maybe there you can find Quersey."

Just as Jacob said, a three-masted schooner sat docked on a sandbar four miles below the city. Gabriel watched the comings and goings of the *Mary* before he moved to board. He recognized the slave Billy. His name had never appeared on Gabriel's list or Sam Byrd's or Solomon's.

Never seen Billy anywhere near the business. Gabriel hesitated to show his face but knew he could not turn back. He waded into the water, and with his bayonet and his sword held high above his head, he requested to board. Billy nodded for Gabriel to throw down his weapons.

My reward is posted all over town. Does Billy remember me?

"Do I know you?" Billy asked. "Aren't you Gabriel? Aren't they lookin' for you?"

Gabriel had given up on receiving any help from Ma's Lord, but still he looked to heaven again, as he always did when he needed a way out. *Daniel,* he thought. *Ma always called me Daniel.* So he told Billy, "I'm Daniel, not Gabriel, but I know who you mean. I'm not that man."

Billy took Gabriel aboard. Captain Taylor promised to get him safely to Norfolk. "I owe a debt to Jacob Kent," Taylor said. "He took me in and got me straightened out. I owe him, and I expect you do, too."

For the whole of the journey, Gabriel stayed belowdeck so as not to be seen by any man on any ship or boat. He hardly ate. He hardly slept, and he spoke to no one.

CHAPTER THIRTY-TWO
September 12–23, 1800

To His Excellency
the Governor of the Commonwealth of Virginia

September 12, 1800
9:00 p.m.
Richmond Jail

Sir,
  I conceive it my unbounded Duty to inclose
Solomon's Petition to Your Excellency — much good
seems to flow from a rapid Execution — my day light
Bell no sooner gave signal to my servants to rise to duty,
than it roused the unfortunate criminals to a sense of
their approaching Fate, and the whole Jail was alive
to Hymns of Praise to the great God and here (I hope)
penitence instantly began.

  Wm. Rose.

PETITION FOR SOLOMON

The Petition of the Negro man Solomon, now under sentence of death in the Jail of Richmond, Humbly represents That the petitioner would consider it as a favour of the highest importance, and as essential to his eternal welfare, if he could possibly, by Your Excellency's goodness, obtain a respite for a few days from the execution of the just and awful sentence which has been pronounced agt. him; that this act of mercy and compassion will not only be of the utmost advantage to the petitioner, but it may ultimately promote the interest of the Commonwealth, as he is ready, if time shall be allowed to him for recollection, to make numerous and important discoveries concerning the late atrocious Conspiracy.

CONFESSION OF SOLOMON

My brother Gabriel was the one who influenced me to join him and others so we might conquer the white people and take their property. When I asked how, he said by falling upon them in the dead of night, at a time they would be unguarded and unsuspicious.

When I asked who would lead it, he said a man from Caroline who was at the siege of Yorktown, and who was to meet him at the water — the Brook — and from there on to Richmond. They would take the city. This man from Caroline was to be in charge the first day, and then, after exercising the soldiers, the commander would be Gabriel. Every Sunday, my brother came to Richmond to provide ammunition to some men and to find where the military stores were deposited.

The first places Gabriel intended to attack in Richmond were the Capitol, the Magazine, the Penitentiary, the Governor's house, and the Governor himself. My brother planned the insurrection now because so many soldiers have been discharged in the last one or two months. He said that would make it easier.

Gabriel said if they succeeded, then they would put down the whole of the country where slavery was permitted, but no further than that.

September 12, 1800
J. Monroe to Mayor of Williamsburg
Richmond

Sir,

   I have been advised that Gabriel, the slave who
was at the head of the late conspiracy and intended
insurrection of the slaves, was seen last night in
Hanover enquiring the route to James Town. I give
you this information that patroles may be ordered
to search for him, since if due exertion be made it
is probable he will be apprehended. I send you his
description that it may be made known as generally as
circumstances will permit in the lower country. I will
thank you to communicate the above to the commanding
officers of the regiment in James City, and likewise
to Mr. Ambler at James Town, with whose slaves
he is probably acquainted. Any expence attending a
compliance with this request will be defrayed by the
publick.

   With great respect I am, Sir,
   J. M.

Virginia Argus, SEPTEMBER 23, 1800, NORFOLK

NOTICE

Gabriel is twenty-four years of age, six feet, two or three inches high, darkish complexion, long visage, with a gloomy insidious brow, short black knotty hair, some scars on his head. Thomas H. Prosser.

CHAPTER THIRTY-THREE
September 24–30, 1800

HE MADE IT TO THE OCEAN. At Norfolk, Gabriel asked to go on deck; he wanted to look out at the sea.

Captain Taylor advised him otherwise. "Stay put for now. That ocean will be there when Quersey arrives. You best keep from the light of day."

Gabriel stayed low; Taylor sent Billy into town to find the Frenchman. Quersey never showed.

The arrest happened quickly and without warning. Billy returned with two constables. The constables boarded the *Mary* and headed straight to Gabriel's bunk. Captain Taylor hardly had time to concoct a story, and the one he offered convinced no one. "I—I was just belowdeck writing you a letter, Constable. To tell you of my prisoner."

The Norfolk men arrested Captain Taylor, too. They shackled Gabriel at his ankles, with his hands bound behind him. Constable Obediah Gunn seized Gabriel's papers—his letter from Quersey and another man from Philadelphia, the roll of names of soldiers from all across Virginia and into North Carolina, and the leaflet on which Nanny had written, for the first time, her name beside his. "Now it's in writing," she had said. *"Nanny and Gabriel."*

Billy stood on the dock, watching, ready to spend his reward.

The Lord, He throws no mercy my way. The business is done.

The men chained and ironed Gabriel, then took him before the mayor of Norfolk. He told nothing to his captors but said only, "I will speak to His Excellency, Governor Monroe. No one else."

My only chance to see Nanny again is to get back to Richmond. If I am tried here in Norfolk, we have no chance.

When he returned to the capital, under guard, Gabriel found that a great crowd waited for him by the river. Some jeered and threw cabbages and squash. Others—Jacob, Mrs. Barnett, and the laundresses—walked with him up the hill to the governor's mansion. The washerwomen sang, and their song lifted Gabriel up. They knew Gabriel, and they knew that his heart was at work not only for himself and Nan but for them, too. These women had showed him all about the creek and the river and taught him how to move about the city and hire out in his trade.

For these true companions, Gabriel felt grateful, but the one face he needed most he did not see. He searched the streets of Richmond for Nanny, and she was not among those at the river, along the hill, or on the capitol grounds.

So massive was the crowd that the governor appeared on his porch, and upon seeing the gathering of black and white residents that had accompanied Gabriel, the terrified Monroe gave an order for fifteen or twenty men to surround Gabriel and remove him to the penitentiary.

From the crowd came cries to free Gabriel and shouts to hang him. The people asked for liberty, and they also asked for death. "Hang General Gabriel!" they cried. "Free the Black General!" they implored. The governor turned his back to all of the people and would not look at Gabriel.

"Inside the mansion, Governor Monroe's young son is dying," remarked one of the guards.

Ma's Lord, He shows no mercy, Gabriel thought.

September 24, 1800
Thomas Newton to the Governor
Norfolk

Excellency,

The bearers of this letter bring with them Negro Gabriel, taken from on board the three-masted schooner Mary, Richard Taylor, Captain, belonging to Richmond. It appears that Taylor left Richmond on Saturday night week and run aground on a bar 4 miles below Richmond.

On Sunday morning, Gabriel hailed the Mary and was brought on board by one of the Negroes on board. The villain was armed with a bayonet fixed on a stick, which he threw into the river. Captain Taylor says he was unwell and in his cabin when Gabriel was brought on board. Negro Billy says he was asleep, and when he awakened and found Gabriel on board, he questioned him. Gabriel said that his name was Daniel.

Capt. Taylor says that Gabriel came on board as a freeman, that he asked him for his papers but he did not shew any, saying he had left them; Capt. Taylor is an old inhabitant, been an overseer, & must have known that neither free blacks nor Slaves could travel in this Country without papers & he certainly must

have had many oppertunities of securing Gabriel.
In the eleven days Gabriel was on board the Mary,
Captain Taylor passed Osborne's Bermuda Hundred,
City Point, and, I suppose, many vessels where he
could have obtained force to have secured Gabriel.
Taylor's conduct after arriving here in Norfolk is
also blamable. Mary *was boarded by a Captain*
Inchman just below here, but Taylor never mentioned
Gabriel. Even after he came up to town, he went
alongside a ship with 25 men on board and never
mentioned the matter.

When he was on shore, Negro Billy mentioned the
matter to a boy by the name of Norris, a blacksmith.
Norris told a Mr. Woodward, who immediately took
such steps to send two constables on board the Schooner
Mary, *where they took him. Gabriel was at liberty on*
board and might have made his escape.

Mr. Taylor must have known & undoubtedly have
heard of Gabriel before he left Richmond. I hope, for
the sake of his family, Taylor may be able to clear
himself of the opinion entertained of him here.

Gabriel says he will give your Excy. a full
information, he will confess to no one else. He will
set off this day under a guard, in a vessel & probably

will reach Osborne's by Friday or Saturday. Should Your Excy. think proper, a guard may be sent Down the River & take him by land, but they will proceed by water as fast as possible & I believe there will be no danger of a rescue.

I am with the greatest respect, Yr. Excy.'s Obt. Servt.,
    Thos. Newton
    Sheriff

ORDERS TO EXECUTIVE COUNCIL
from GOVERNOR JAMES MONROE,
Respecting Gabriel, SEPTEMBER 28, 1800

THIS slave Gabriel was brought to my house yesterday about 4 o'clock in the afternoon, and, a great cloud of blacks as well as whites gathering round him, I requested Captain Giles, who was present, to form a guard of 15 or 20 of the citizens he could collect on the ground, and take him under its care to the Penitentiary and continue to guard him there with that number of men in a separate cell till further orders, holding no conversation with him on any subject or permitting any other person to do so.

GABRIEL BACK IN RICHMOND

On Saturday last, the noted Gabriel appeared here by water, under guard from Norfolk. He was taken before the Governor, and after some interrogations, committed to the Penitentiary, for trial: We understand that when he was apprehended, he manifested the greatest marks of firmness and composure, showing not the least disposition to equivocate, or scream himself from justice. He denied the charge of being the first, in exciting the insurrection, although he was to have had the chief command — but, that there were four or five persons more materially concerned in the conspiracy; and said that he could mention several in Norfolk.

We have heard it highly rumoured, that he has letters in his possession from white people, but do not intend to set it forth as a report deserving of credit; we only wish it may be true, provided there are white men in the plot that they may be brought to justice.

CHAPTER THIRTY-FOUR
October 1800

THE TRIAL OF GABRIEL, 6 OCTOBER 1800

WITNESS, PROSSER'S BEN:

"Gabriel was appointed Captain at first and when he had enlisted a number of men was appointed General. They were to kill Mr. Prosser and Mr. Mosby and all the neighbors, and then proceed to Richmond, where they would kill everybody, take the treasury, and divide the money. If the White people agreed to their freedom, they would hoist a White flag, and Gabriel would dine and drink with the merchants of the City, on the day when it should be so agreed. He enlisted a number of men and made them swords. He made the handles to the swords which were made by Solomon and showed

me nearly a peck of bullets, which he and Martin had run. He said he had 10 pounds of powder which he had purchased. He said he had nearly 10,000 men — 1,000 in Richmond, about 600 in Caroline, and nearly 500 at the Coal Pits, besides others at different places. Gabriel expected the poor White people would join him. Two Frenchmen did join, but those names he would not tell. Gabriel enlisted nearly all the Negroes in town. He said amongst them he had 400 Horsemen. He said all the Negroes from Petersburg were to join him after he had commenced the Insurrection."

WITNESS, MR. PRICE'S JOHN:

"I saw Gabriel at a meeting. He invited the men to come to the spring to drink grog. When I got there, he mentioned the War against the white people. He said all us men should join him and meet him in three weeks to start the business."

WITNESS, BEN WOOLFOLK:

"Gabriel held at a meeting at Mr. Young's. He came to get men to join him to carry on the War against the white people. Gabriel said he had twelve dozen swords made and had worn out two pair of Bullet moulds in running bullets. He had a third pair in *his pocket, nearly worn out. He said Bob Cooley and Mr. Tinsley's Jim was to let him into the Capitol to get the arms and that Rocketts was to be fired, to draw away the Citizens and give him a chance to seize on the arms and ammunition. He said when they came back, then they would attack them.*

"I was there when Gabriel was appointed General. None were to be spared of the Whites except Quakers, Methodists, and French people. That was the plan. Gabriel and Gilbert went to purchase a piece of Silk for a flag and they were to write on it, Death or liberty. *They said they would kill all unless they agreed to the freedom."*

IT IS THE UNANIMOUS OPINION OF THE COURT THAT THE SAID NEGRO MAN SLAVE GABRIEL IS GUILTY OF THE CRIME WITH WHICH HE STANDS ACCUSED AND FOR THE SAME THAT HE BE HANGED BY THE NECK UNTIL HE BE DEAD AND THAT EXECUTION OF THIS SENTENCE BE DONE AND PERFORMED ON HIM, THE SAID GABRIEL, ON TOMORROW AT THE USUAL PLACE OF EXECUTION. HANG HIM BY THE NECK TILL HE BE DEAD DEAD DEAD.

CHAPTER THIRTY-FIVE
October 10, 1800

NANNY WAITED in the forest. On the morning Gabriel was set to hang, she arrived first to the woods behind Prosser's Tavern, not far from Brookfield. Five men would die—Gabriel, Sam Byrd, George, Frank, and Gilbert. Word had quickly reached Henrico that Gabriel had petitioned the court to hang with his men in the countryside instead of alone at the gallows near the market house in Richmond.

Will they tie four ropes or five? Nanny wondered. *Will I see Gabriel today, or will he die alone in Richmond?*

The morning was clear and cool, the kind of autumn day that smells of a long-ago summer yet hints, too, at the long, suffering winter to come. The birds and rodents of the woods paid Nanny's presence among them no mind but went about the business of foraging and burrowing and watching with her. The patrollers, assembling a makeshift gallows, paid Nanny no mind either.

She watched them to know if her husband would die alone. *Four ropes or five?* The sudden stillness of the child she carried or the empty quickening of the moment turned her queasy.

She found herself praying that Gabriel would hang there at Prosser's Tavern and not in the city. She wanted to see him; she wanted to stand near him, sing to him, and sit by his body, caressing him until she was certain he had passed over.

Let them tie five ropes. This was how Nanny prayed to see Gabriel. *If this is to be our end, let them tie for five men. Let me stand in witness. Lord, let him hear my voice.*

All the people from all the quarters gathered in the field by the tavern; their owners encouraged them to go and watch, gave them time free from work so that they could witness the state exacting its price.

When the patrollers tied but four ropes, Nanny knew. The fifth rope was being tied in Richmond. Her husband would hang alone at the Fifteenth Street gallows. They would put his body in the side of the hill, where they laid all the dead slaves of Richmond. She would never find him.

They will build the city over him, she thought, and then the idea seized upon Nanny that if she ran, she could reach Gabriel. *I will get to him within the hour. I will reach through the bars of the cart and run along beside him through the streets and not let go his hand until they peel me away. I'll climb up the scaffold and take hold of his feet. Let them bury me and our child with him in the hill.*

But Nanny carried no remit pass, and the road to Richmond swarmed with militia. No one from the countryside dared leave now without a pass, especially those known to have been involved in the business, and though the hangings were said to be coming to an end, Nanny had been implicated by the testimony of her dear, and now dead, friend Isaac.

When the cart came with Sam and George and Frank and Gilbert but without Gabriel to the hanging trees near Prosser's Tavern, Nanny stepped into the crowd and made her way to the front. She was sure from where she stood, she could hear the roar of another crowd six miles away.

In town at the gallows, they are cheering him! The people are cheering General Gabriel, Nanny imagined.

The hangman's cart drove away, leaving the boys of the business to dangle from the live-oak limbs. Nanny raised her fist to heaven. "Death or liberty!" she cried out. *Let them take me and my child, too,* Nanny thought, but no one did.

As Nanny witnessed the four men fall, she witnessed Gabriel fall four times over. *Whether his name is Sam or George or Gilbert or Frank, his name is also Gabriel.*

She would not turn away when Sam's feet jerked up or when George's body spun in tight circles. Once the people left, Nanny remained. "Cut them loose. I will care for them." She pointed to Gilbert, the youngest and smallest of the four bodies hanging, then climbed into the cart driven by Pleasant Younghusband.

The coroner started to protest, but the old colonel nodded his permission for Nanny to tend the bodies. Nanny was determined that if she could not wash Gabriel and sing to him and draw his face, she would do so for Sam, George, Gilbert, and Frank. She would not abandon the business; she could not abandon these boys.

In the days immediately following the hangings,

Nanny didn't remember seeing four soldiers die. She stored the memory of execution day, watching Gabriel die over and over and over and over. Her mind's eye let repeat how Gabriel's body had twirled round and round. Long after he should have swayed to a stop, the early autumn wind kept him moving.

Nanny had thought she might lose the child from her grief. At night when she rolled over in the bed and went to drape her leg across Gabriel's, finding him gone, the ache in Nanny's chest moved up to her throat, then down to her womb.

The thought of letting go, going home, and falling forever into the crater left by Gabriel's absence brought Nanny some relief. She imagined her surrender to someplace far away from Richmond and beyond even the trees, into the great opening that she was certain would reunite her with her husband. She longed to go there, to the good and right world where Gabriel had by now arrived and where their child still waited—the place of all beginnings and all endings. Nanny imagined how she might release herself from this life.

Yet the seductive ease, the rush of release, that might come of a quick death by her own hand frightened Nanny. So she went to the still side of the hill near the spring, where she and Gabriel used to sit. She invited the wind to move through her womb. The child pushed an elbow into Nanny's side, and this kept her alive.

CHAPTER THIRTY-SIX
April 1801

Colonel Nathaniel Wilkinson
Births

~

Hannah and Cate born about March 1790.
Gave them to John.

Lilly had a daughter born the tenth of June,
1795. Named Mahalia.
Another—Becca, October 1798.

Amy—a son named——, born December 1795.
Died the eleventh.
Another son, Jacob. November 2, 1796.

Lilly, a son named Peter. February 8, 1797.
Died October 1798.

Sall Amy's daughter had a daughter, Esther,
born July 20, 1798.
And a son, Abram.

Lilly, another son, John, May 15, 1799.

Nanny had a son, Daniel. Born of her husband,
Gabriel. April 1801.

NANNY COULD NEVER FORGET Gabriel's face or his voice or the way his hand felt around her waist. After the hangings, after dozens of men died for liberty, the state had made its practice to banish those involved in the business. Many men were sent away from Virginia, far away south, to Georgia, Kentucky, and South Carolina, places Nan did not wish to go. Her child grew and stirred and made ready to come, but still Nanny could not say, *It's all right, it's all right.*

When she needed to find some part of her husband, she would stop to sit beneath Gabriel's apple tree on her way to worship or after her work was done for the night. There, she dug a new space in the ground — not deep or wide, like the place near the market in the city that claimed Gabriel's decaying body and bones. Not eternally empty, like the space left in her heart. She reached into her pocket for the apple seeds. She placed them, a bunch of three, together into the earth and patted down the dirt. The ground here was good now, and the weather very fine, like summer.

Again Nanny slipped her hand into her apron. She pulled her husband's paper and inkwell and pen from her other pocket. The scent of Gabriel still lingered in the fibers of the cotton-rag paper. She wrote her name and Gabriel's side by side. She touched the written-down truth in her hand: *Nanny and Gabriel.*

There on the hill, while the baby waited for his day and the April breeze pledged sweetness by August, Nanny sat beneath the tree that knew and remembered him. Wafting up from Young's orchard, the wind delivered the promise of persimmon and apple and plum and pear. The yellow warblers at meadow's edge revealed to her the invisible trace that would lead her to him whenever she needed him most.

Isaac, Venus, Jupiter. Solomon, Martin, Ma. They carried Nanny to Gabriel, to the place where she could hear Gabriel's true and free spirit singing the songs of his beautiful people, urging them on, firing their courage, steeling their resolve. She could hear her husband awakening his beautiful people with his steady anvil beat.

Ping, ping, ping. Gabriel, forging together their spirits. *Ping, ping, ping.* Gabriel, making freedom.

From all the earth and in all the trees, from the creek and on the wind, all the people who had passed back over and all those waiting to come in joined their voices with Gabriel's. They sang and cried. Made praise, made promise.

Beneath their tree, Nanny heard him. *Come freedom, come freedom. Freedom go on and come.*

Every fall during the three years I spent writing *Come August, Come Freedom*, I visited the eleventh-grade U.S. history classes at Saint Gertrude's, an all-girls high school in my hometown of Richmond, Virginia. History teacher Nancy Rives and I created a Gabriel module that includes an original song written and performed by Mrs. Rives and an overview of the insurrection plot with maps, trial excerpts, and discussion. The questions raised by the students were similar from class to class, year to year: *Is this a true story? How much is true? What happened to Nanny? Where did all of this happen? Why did you write this story? How much do we really know?*

When you finish reading *Come August, Come Freedom*, I encourage you to read the public documents and historical works about Gabriel's Insurrection. Come visit Richmond. Sit at Young's Spring and quiet your mind. Stand near I-95, down the hill from the Virginia state capitol building, and know that Gabriel and many enslaved people from centuries past are buried below the pavement, the cobblestone, and the clay.

Come here and make a pilgrimage of reconciliation. Stand where Gabriel stood and find your easy breath.

When you reach your innermost stillness, just observe: What do you hear in your heart? How do you imagine Gabriel and Nan? Find a way to tell someone else how the story speaks to you. Tweet it. Make a collage. Write a song. Write a play. Draw a portrait. Pick up your guitar. Pick up your pencil. Pick up your hammer.

How much do we really know? The public record about Gabriel's life reveals just a few facts about his twenty-four years. We know he was a blacksmith and that he had two brothers and a wife, for example. For the most part, Gabriel's thoughts, feelings, and motivations related to his family and even the rebellion itself remain inaccessible, except through imagining.

For us to imagine or meditate upon Gabriel's life inevitably means that we meld our own life experiences with the limited pool of available facts about him. So it's a true thing to say about this book that after all my researching and even with all I've learned and know, maybe I'm wrong about what really happened. Maybe I'm wrong about who Gabriel and Nan were.

But based on what we do know and after all the time and thought I've given to their story, Gabriel and Nanny remind me that, every day, we are each called to rise and pursue life, liberty, and happiness. They also remind me that none of us is free until all of us are free.

Thank you so much for reading my book,

Is this a true story? How much is true?

The public historical record speaks primarily to the court proceedings surrounding Gabriel's trials of 1799 and 1800, and those sources present Gabriel through the filter of the state authorities who condemned and executed him. Altogether, the trial documents illuminate barely a year of his life.

A Commonwealth of Virginia tax record confirms that Gabriel lived at Brookfield, a two-thousand-acre tobacco plantation in Henrico County, about six miles north of Richmond, the capital of Virginia. Gabriel's two brothers, Martin and Solomon, also lived there. For most of Gabriel's life, a planter named Thomas Prosser owned Brookfield. In *Gabriel's Rebellion: The Virginia Slave Conspiracies of 1800 & 1802* (1993), Douglas Egerton reports that Thomas Prosser's tax roll of 1783 lists all three brothers; Gabriel would have been about seven years old. This tax record is located at the Library of Virginia and it lists Gabriel, Solomon, and Martin as among those who were enslaved at Brookfield. Testimony from the insurrection trials confirms Martin and Solomon as Gabriel's brothers. I have followed Egerton's suggestion that Martin was the oldest by far, Solomon the middle brother, and Gabriel the youngest.

Brookfield is no longer standing, though a Mutual Assurance insurance policy drawing from 1806 shows how the house likely looked during Gabriel's lifetime. The property was up the hill from a creek called Brook Run, which empties into the Chickahominy Swamp. When Thomas passed away, on October 7, 1798, his son, Thomas Henry, inherited the plantation.

In *Gabriel's Rebellion*, Egerton concludes that Gabriel was born in 1776 when he references a statement given by Thomas Henry Prosser in September of 1800 that Gabriel was at the time twenty-four years old. Gabriel and Thomas Henry Prosser were the same age—both born in 1776—Thomas Henry on November 5th of that year.

It seems likely to me that the two boys would have played together, found trouble together, and maybe even slept in the same room in the main house on occasion. Slave narratives and eyewitness accounts, such as *We Lived in a Little Cabin in the Yard*, edited by Belinda Hurmence, describe how young children—black and white—played together on plantations. Some accounts describe how white children denied the bonds of friendship as they stepped into the role of master or mistress and went from protesting the whipping of slaves to ordering it themselves.

The public historical record doesn't directly identify Gabriel's parents, so I referred to works by Belinda Hurmence, Jacqueline Jones, James Sidbury, and Lorena Walsh to ignite my imagination about Gabriel's family, family life in slave quarters, and the roles of women in post-colonial Virginia. Egerton conjectures that Gabriel's mother may have been African-born.

Robert King Carter, one of the wealthiest planters in Virginia, may have owned as many as one thousand slaves at the time of his death in 1732. My understanding of the patterns of slavery in Virginia in the 1700s is that it often involved white men, such as Carter and Prosser, selling slaves within the state. In fact, Prosser did place a notice in the *Virginia Gazette* in 1770, advertising seven slaves for sale in Cumberland County. Reflecting on all of this, I fabricated a set of parents for Gabriel, with Pa being Virginia-born and Gabriel's paternal grandfather a captive African king purchased by Thomas Prosser from Robert King Carter. I created Ma as an African-born woman sold into slavery in Richmond.

Did young slaves from the countryside apprentice with white blacksmiths in the city?

I took that question to the Virginia Historical Society, and, in the book *The Virginia Negro Artisans and Tradesmen* (1926) by Raymond Bennett Pinchbeck, found data to support my plot idea of sending Solomon and Gabriel to apprentice with Jacob Kent. Whether Gabriel apprenticed at Brookfield or in Richmond, I don't know, but I wanted to get him to the city as soon as possible and under the influence of the river, the laundresses, and freedom-minded men like the fictional Jacob Kent. I wanted the city to be Gabriel's transformative world.

Who taught Gabriel to read?

The reward notice issued for Gabriel, testimony in the 1800 trials, and oral tradition concur that Gabriel could read and write. Someone educated Gabriel. Was it Ann Prosser? I found an old Richmond newspaper article from the 1890s (ninety years after the events) that printed the oral history of Gabriel's Rebellion and mentioned that Brookfield's mistress taught him to read. In essays written in the early 1930s, Gabriel's literacy is also attributed to the mistress of Brookfield. Did she really teach him to read? No record on this exists, only a couple hundred years of folks speculating that it was Ann Prosser. On this question, I stuck with tradition and assigned Ann Prosser her own act of resistance.

Did Gabriel really bite off Absalom Johnson's ear?

Yes. Court evidence from 1799 (the pig incident) and 1800 (the insurrection) shows that Gabriel frequently socialized with a man named Jupiter, who lived at the farm next door to Brookfield and was enslaved by Colonel Nathaniel Wilkinson. Wilkinson rented out land, Jupiter, and other people to Absalom Johnson, a newcomer to Henrico County from the more rural Dinwiddie County, where Johnson had worked as an overseer. Jupiter, Solomon, and Gabriel did steal a pig; Gabriel did bite off "a considerable part" of Absalom Johnson's left ear. For Gabriel, maiming was a capital offense punishable by death, but in 1799 Gabriel was spared death at the gallows by invoking benefit of clergy, a sort of loophole that existed in Virginia law for slaves charged with capital crimes, excluding insurrection. To learn more about the benefit of clergy and criminal law and slavery, consult *Twice Condemned: Slaves & the Criminal Laws of Virginia, 1705–1865* (1988) by Philip J. Schwarz. The 1799 trial documents do not identify which Bible verse Gabriel recited; the verse I gave

Gabriel was a continuation of the Psalm invoked by Ma in chapter two. For all Bible verses, I used the *New Jerusalem Bible* because it's the translation that I read and has the contemporary flavor that felt right to me for this story.

There's no evidence to guide us in knowing exactly why the young men went to steal the pig that day, so I fabricated motives for the theft and for Gabriel's branding of Absalom Johnson forevermore as one-eared Absalom Johnson. Insurrection trial testimony describes gatherings of slaves from neighboring farms to worship, to celebrate, to mourn, and to reunite with family and friends. Court testimony surrounding the insurrection trials of 1800 references Prosser's Tavern, Young's Spring, Brook's Bridge, Littlepage Bridge, and Half Sink as important gathering places for the community of enslaved people in the neighborhood of Brookfield. This all led me to imagine that Gabriel needed the pig for his wedding feast, since I wanted this book to be, in part, a love story between Gabriel and Nanny. While the 1799 trial records indicate that Gabriel and Absalom did scuffle before Gabriel bit off the farmer's ear, the records give no hint as to what words were exchanged between them. I gave Johnson the villainous task of exploiting his perceived power over Gabriel by threatening Nanny.

Was Gabriel's wife really named Nanny? Where did she live? What happened to her?

The public record doesn't reveal too much about Nanny. Some secondary sources refer to her as Nancy. On the 1783 Brookfield tax roll, there is no slave listed as Nanny. In my research, which was not an exhaustive effort to find every enslaved woman name Nanny or Nancy in the region, I twice encountered documentation (other than the court transcripts) of an enslaved female named Nanny living in the nearby vicinity of Brookfield during the early 1800s. The written rental agreement between Absalom Johnson and Colonel Wilkinson itemizes the land and slaves that the Colonel rented to Johnson. Among the slaves: Old Jupiter and what appeared to me to read Nanny. I also saw an 1803 reference to a Nanny of childbearing age in the slave logs of the Tinsley family at Totomoi in Hanover County. Were these the same Nanny? Are either of these women Gabriel's wife? I don't have those answers. While the trial documents do implicate Nanny and confirm her involvement in the plot, I am not aware that she or any woman was brought to trial in 1800. In June 2012, *Richmond* magazine published "The Blood of Gabriel: Reaching to the roots of a slave rebellion" by Harry Kollatz Jr., which, for the first time that I'm aware of, records the family history of Gabriel as told by Haskell Bingham, a descendant of Gabriel's and the current family historian.

When did Gabriel start planning the rebellion?
The public record of Gabriel's life indicates that he spent a month in the Richmond jail after being found guilty of maiming Johnson. He was released to Thomas Henry Prosser on November 5, 1799. (Thomas Henry Prosser spent his twenty-third birthday at the jail and the courthouse bailing out Gabriel and appearing before the court to swear that Gabriel would act "peacefully toward all the good people.")

The testimony surrounding the 1800 plan for freedom says that Gabriel started planning for the rebellion—even making weapons—shortly after the "last harvest," though the year is not indicated. By June of 1800, plans were well under way. Trial witnesses place Gabriel, at different times throughout the summer of 1800, in Henrico, Hanover, Richmond, and Caroline. His recruits testified that he and Solomon were making weapons and that he and Martin were forging bullets. Gabriel also had money in his pocket. He gave money to Ben Woolfolk and Sam Byrd to buy grog for men around the region during recruiting missions.

According to testimony, sometime in August, a few weeks before the insurrection was to take place, Gabriel's men held an election between Gabriel and another enslaved man named Jack Ditcher. They voted Gabriel as their general by a large margin, and at the same meeting voted to initiate "the business" on the evening of Saturday, August 30th. Two things interfered with that plan.

First, a tremendous storm came up from the west and flooded the countryside and the city. Diaries and correspondence say it was a once-in-a-lifetime storm. Governor James Monroe wrote that every living thing sought shelter from it. Two hundred and four years later to the day, Richmonders felt the wrath of such a storm when Tropical Storm Gaston parked over the city and dropped fourteen inches of rain in eight hours, leaving more than a dozen people dead and bridges and roads washed out all over town. In 2004, during Gaston, there was no moving about in the daylight; we were a city at the mercy of the weather.

On August 30, 1800, Gabriel, Solomon, and Nanny ran from quarter to quarter, rescheduling the insurrection for Sunday night—same time, different date and different place. They had no idea that even as they were busy delaying "the business," Governor Monroe had already been informed. Two enslaved men—Pharoah and Tom—had betrayed the insurrection and named Gabriel as its leader. Private patrollers ventured out into the storm but discovered nothing. By the next day, the militia had descended upon Brookfield and neighboring farms. Gabriel and Jack Ditcher escaped; Ditcher eventually turned himself in to the authorities in Richmond. Gabriel made it to Norfolk before being apprehended there, shackled, and transported upriver back to Richmond.

What did Gabriel look like?

Virginia's official description of Gabriel and Thomas Henry Prosser's statement describe Gabriel in terms not only of his size, stature, and complexion but also the markings on his body: missing teeth and scars on his forehead. The proclamation issued by the Commonwealth in September 1800 states, "Gabriel is a Negro of a brown complexion, about six feet, three or four inches high, a bony face, well made, and very active, he has two or three scars on his head, his hair is very short, and has lost two front teeth."

Slave narratives and eyewitness accounts document that slave owners commonly inflicted people held in their captivity with distinguishing marks so that if they ran away it would be easier to identify and capture them. This abuse was also a mechanism for humiliation, domination, and physical and psychological control. The record omits the details of how Gabriel lost his teeth or why his forehead had marks, but I chose to use these physical traits of Gabriel—which are the types of body marks described in slave narratives—to illustrate the abhorrent practice of one class of people marking ownership over another.

Are all of the characters in the book real people?
The characters in *Come August, Come Freedom* include those inspired by real people and those entirely fabricated. Many, many men—by some accounts, tens of thousands—joined Gabriel's army. The trial documents list two different Gabriels, two Solomons, several Toms and Bens, and dozens more men. In my early drafts, I included a character named and modeled after Gabriel's coleader, Jack Ditcher, but I found that his presence distracted from what I wanted to be primarily a story about love and family. I did fabricate a few characters completely. Jacob Kent, Pa, and Ma are totally imaginary, as are Old Major, Kissey, and Venus.

Why did you create fictional secondary characters at all? Why not just use the historical figures as the basis for the story?
The court records indicate that the actual plot involved mostly men and, to me, this story felt like it was about family, love, marriage, and the insistence to engage in family life freely and by choice. Nanny is the only woman named in the actual trial documents, other than a few widowed slave owners whose names were recorded as a means of identifying

their slaves and compensating them once those men were put to death or sent out of state. Yet more than just needing women in the story, I wanted to create for Gabriel a sort of lineage of self-determination by showing all sorts of acts of resistance and insistence undertaken by the men and women in his family and his community.

The diary entries of Thomas Prosser, sprinkled through the book, reflect only the words and thoughts of my fictionalized Thomas Prosser. I fabricated these entries and leaned on the language and cadence of the personal diaries of the Tinsley family in Hanover, Virginia. A Tinsley descendant lives on her family's farm, the former Totomoi plantation. The main house and land have changed very little since the late 1700s. My sister arranged for me to spend an afternoon there, reading through diaries, old tax records, the family bible, and an invoice for a year's worth of blacksmith jobs that kept the farm in working order. These documents and the hours spent at Totomoi helped me imagine certain details about life at Brookfield: how the weather was unbearable for Prosser, yet the "hands" still worked in the fields; Prosser's dependence on Kissey and Old Major; and his indulgence of Thomas Henry. I can't say enough how deeply those hours spent at Totomoi inspired me.

How much about Gabriel's capture is true?

On the night of August 30, 1800, Gabriel's plans unraveled due to the big storm and the betrayal of two enslaved men—Pharaoh Sheppard and Tom. Even as the storm approached, Mosby Sheppard was hearing of the plot from

Pharoah and Tom. As Gabriel, Nanny, Solomon, Jupiter, and Sam Byrd ran from quarter to quarter, postponing the rising until Sunday night, Virginia Governor James Monroe was rousing the militia. Gabriel disappeared from Brookfield sometime on Sunday, August 31st. The record next places him on September 11th in Hanover County, asking about passage to Jamestown. (Four slaves associated with Hanover Tavern, which is still in operation, participated in the plot.) Governor Monroe circulated a reward notice and Gabriel's description in newspapers. News of the plot traveled not only throughout the state of Virginia but as far north as Philadelphia and as far south as North Carolina and Mississippi.

During this crisis of his term, Monroe sought the advice of Thomas Jefferson. John Adams's slanderer, James Callender, wrote to Jefferson about the insurrection, too. From the Richmond jail, where he was being held on charges stemming from violation of the Sedition Act, Callender had a firsthand view of the unfolding events because the same jail held Gabriel's men. In early drafts, I included extracts from letters to and from Thomas Jefferson but found that the letters detracted from the personal story of Gabriel. Known as the Thomas Jefferson Papers, the correspondence is accessible online at the Library of Congress as part of the American Memory Collection.

Gabriel did hitch a ride on the *Mary* with former overseer, Richard Taylor. When he first waded into the river, the slave Billy recognized Gabriel and said something to the effect of: *Aren't you Gabriel, the one they're after?* Gabriel replied that he was called Gabriel but that his name was really Daniel. In all that I read, I believe this is the one of the final records of Gabriel speaking, so it was important to me to explore this statement from him. Was Gabriel speaking in code? Was he invoking scripture or sending a message as the biblical Daniel did: *I am not divine; I am a man.* The trial records of 1799 where Gabriel invoked his benefit of clergy speak to Gabriel's familiarity with the bible. He was able to recite a verse from memory. Trial testimony describes how Gabriel's brother Martin spoke of the book of Exodus and demonstrated a familiarity with scripture. (Biblical scholar and award-winning author Kristin Swenson helped me think about the parallels between Gabriel and Daniel. At her suggestion, I turned to the *Jewish Study Bible* to further study the book of Daniel.)

The schooner *Mary* reached Norfolk, where Billy went ashore and turned in Gabriel to the local authorities. I included the letter from Thomas Newton, the sheriff of Norfolk, because this is a primary-source description of Gabriel's return. I also read other accounts of Gabriel's capture, namely newspaper articles and a journal entry of John Boyce on film at the Library of Virginia. Boyce, a planter in Henrico, had dined with Mr. Young—presumably Mr. Young of Westbrook, the site of Young's Spring—the night before Gabriel's return to Richmond. Boyce noted in his journal that it was a cold, gray, rainy day when Gabriel arrived back in Richmond and was taken before the governor.

Gabriel was hanged at the 15th Street gallows in Richmond, on October 10, 1800. That same day, four of his men were hanged near Brookfield at a makeshift gallows. More than two hundred years after Gabriel's hanging, the Virginia Chapter of the National Association for the Advancement of Colored People sought to restore Gabriel's place in history by asking the Commonwealth of Virginia to pardon him. On August 30, 2007, Virginia governor Timothy Kaine informally pardoned Gabriel, stating that "Gabriel's cause—the end of slavery—and the furtherance of equality of all people—has prevailed in the light of history."

When did you first learn about Gabriel?

I only remember learning about Gabriel's Rebellion in 1998, when I happened upon Spring Park in Henrico County. At the time, I lived just up the hill in Richmond's Bellevue neighborhood and had driven down to the bank. Spring Park practically sits in the bank's parking lot. I walked over and read these words: "Adjacent to this park, in a location known as Young's Spring, Gabriel, a slave of Thomas Prosser, was appointed leader of the rebellion in the summer of 1800. He lived on Brookfield Plantation in Henrico County. His objectives were to overtake the capital and convince Governor James Monroe to support more political, social, and economic equality between members of society. Gabriel targeted area slaves, white artisans, freemen, religious supporters and French sympathizers as recruits for his revolution."

Where did all of this happen?

Court testimony states that Gabriel went into Richmond every Sunday to plan, recruit, and gather information. Gabriel's

Richmond was a new city, freshly torn out of the forest, when Virginia moved its capital there from Williamsburg in 1780. In his lifetime, the roads changed from dirt to cobblestone, the houses from wood to brick. The James River and Kanawha Canal was completed and the Spring Street penitentiary built, as was the capitol building itself. Change was the constant factor in Richmond during Gabriel's life.

I used *Ploughshares into Swords: Race, Rebellion, and Identity in Gabriel's Virginia, 1730–1810* by James Sidbury; *The River Where America Began* by Bob Deans; *Facts and Legends of the Hills of Richmond* by Wayne Dementi and Brooks Smith; and *Poe's Richmond* by Agnes M. Bondurant to help me better understand Richmond of the late eighteenth century—the architecture, the topography, the society, the politics, and especially, the river. And even though more than two centuries have passed, I went back to some of the places that informed Gabriel's sense of place. When students ask, "Where did all this take place?", I think they are asking for help in considering their own sense of place and who they must become once they know how their America and Gabriel's intersect.

Why did you write this story?

Many founding heroes, *she*roes, and patriots have become part of America's collective story. Tales of such people teach us something and exemplify the qualities we admire in our great citizens. Gabriel's Rebellion reveals so much of the thinking of our leaders in the early days of America, the rampant liberty fever that was worldwide by 1800, and how enslaved people were engaged in the pursuit of freedom and the call to end slavery long before the Civil War broke out. To me, Gabriel and Nan's story ought to join our larger American story of freedom-loving patriots who lived and sacrificed for our liberty.

Please note that extracts have in some cases been excerpted and/or slightly edited for readability for the modern reader.

p. 9: This is an adaptation of a newspaper ad placed in the *Virginia Gazette*. The actual ad was from Stafford County, about one hour north of Henrico, and the enslaved man was named Charles. I changed the names to reflect Old Major and Henrico County. *Virginia Gazette*, December 2, 1775. http://research.history.org/DigitalLibrary/VirginiaGazette/VGImagePopup.cfm?ID=4641&Res=HI.

pp. 15 and 107: These are fabricated journal entries modeled after the unpublished, privately held plantation journal of John Tinsley in Hanover County written during the same time period. See Tinsley in the bibliography.

p. 36: *Virginia Gazette*, July 10, 1762. http://www.slideshare.net/stratalum/richmonds-slave-trade.

p. 43: This illustration is modeled after a Mutual Assurance insurance drawing of Brookfield from 1806, held by the Henrico County Historical Society. http://www.henricohistoricalsociety.org/lostarchitecture.brookfieldplantation.html.

p. 79: Mary Randolph, *The Virginia Housewife* (Baltimore: Plaskitt, Fite, 1838) 133–134.

p. 92: This is a fabricated blacksmith shop list. I consulted an 1854 blacksmith invoice from the Tinsley family papers and also a James Anderson blacksmith log from the 1790s for the types of jobs Gabriel may have performed at Brookfield, as well as for spelling customs of the period. See Tinsley and Anderson in the bibliography.

p. 130: *Henrico County Order Book*, 94–95.

p. 133: Ibid., 102.

p. 142: Ibid., 105.

pp. 145-146: This leaflet is fabricated in the style of (and based on my extensive reading of) Colonial-era gray propaganda in the form of printed leaflets, pamphlets, and letters. I received confirmation for the notion that abolitionists used the Haitian Revolution to stir anti-slavery sentiment from David Richardson, *Abolition and Its Aftermath: The Historical Context, 1790–1916* (Totowa, NJ: F. Cass, 1985).

pp. 160-161 and 170-171: Executive Papers of Governor James Monroe.

pp. 183-184: Sheppard.

pp. 190 and 197: Executive Papers of Governor James Monroe.

pp. 198-199: Schwarz, *Gabriel's Conspiracy*, 36–37.

pp. 200-201: Flournoy, 141.

p. 205: Ibid., 144–145.

pp. 206–207: Ibid., 147.

p. 208: Schwarz, *Gabriel's Conspiracy*. September 12, 1800 J. Monroe to mayor of Williamsburg: Authentic letter, slightly edited for readability, 48.

p. 209: Ibid, 74.

pp. 213–215: Flournoy, 154–155.

p. 216: Ibid., 156.

p. 217: Schwarz, *Gabriel's Conspiracy*, 135.

pp. 218–220: Flournoy, 165–166.

pp. 227–228: This is fabricated, based on a slave log of the Tinsley family of Hanover, Virginia, kept between the pages of the family Bible, documenting slave births from 1790 to 1804. See Tinsley in the bibliography.

p. 239: "peacefully toward all the good people": *Henrico County Order Book*.

p. 241: "Gabriel is a Negro . . . two front teeth.": Schwarz, *Gabriel's Conspiracy*, 49.

Bibliography

Primary Sources

Anderson, James. *Account Book, 1788–1799.* MS. Virginia Historical Society, Richmond.

Auditor of Public Accounts (1776–1928). Virginia. MS. Misc. Reel 1323. Library of Virginia, Richmond.

Babb, Winston C. *French Refugees from Saint Dominique to the Southern United States.* 1791–1810. MS. Virginia Historical Society, Richmond.

Boyce, John. Journal of John Boyce. 1798–1808. MS. Library of Virginia, Richmond.

Callender, James. Letter to Thomas Jefferson, September 13, 1800. Thomas Jefferson Papers. Library of Congress.

Executive Papers of Governor James Monroe, 1799–1802. MS. Misc. Reels 5332–5350. Library of Virginia, Richmond.

General Asssembly, Virginia. *Letters, Communications, and Evidence, 1800 December 5.* MS. Misc. Reel 5382. Library of Virginia, Richmond.

Gentlemen ___ County. Letter to Editor of *Virginia Herald* (Fredericksburg). September 23, 1800. *Journal of American History,* May 5, 2009.

The Good Old Virginia Almanack, for the Year of Our Lord, 1800. MS. Fiche 131. Library of Virginia, Richmond.

Henrico County Order Book 9 Reel 73. MS. Library of Virginia, Richmond.

Jefferson, Thomas. Letter to James Monroe, September 20, 1800. Thomas Jefferson Papers. Library of Congress.

Kambourian, Elizabeth. *Signs and Sites Pertaining to the Gabriel Slave Conspiracy.* MS. Vertical File: Gabriel Prosser. Virginia Historical Society, Richmond.

Monroe, James. "Oak Hill." Letter to Joseph Carrington Cabel, February 8, 1828. MS. Virginia Historical Society, Richmond.

Mosby, William. Letter to Governor James Monroe, September 1800. Library of Virginia, Richmond. http://www.lva.virginia.org/whoweare/exhibits/DeathLiberty/gabriel/mosby11.htm.

Moss, John. Letter to Governor James Monroe, 1800. Library of Virginia, Richmond. http://www.lva.virginia.org/whoweare/exhibits/DeathLiberty/gabriel/moss16.htm.

Newton, Thomas. Letter to Governor James Monroe, September 24, 1800. Library of Virginia, Richmond. http://www.lva.virginia.org/whoweare/exhibits/DeathLiberty/gabriel/newton14.htm.

Palmer, William P. *Gabriel's Insurrection, 1800.* MS. Virginia Historical Society, Richmond.

Sheppard, Mosby. Letter to Governor James Monroe, August 30, 1800. Library of Virginia, Richmond. http://www.lva.virginia.org/whoweare/exhibits/DeathLiberty/gabriel/sheppard10.htm.

Tinsley, Colonel Thomas Garland, and Thomas Garland Tinsley. Personal papers, 1790–1859. Totopomoi Farm, Hanover, VA.

U.S. State Department. *Trafficking in Persons Report.* Washington, D.C.: Department of State, 2009.

Virginia State Department. *Commonwealth Against Sundry Negroes*. 1800. Library of Virginia, Richmond. http://www.lva.virginia.org/whoweare/exhibits/DeathLiberty/gabriel/commonwealth.htm.

———. *Evidence Adduced Against Solomon the Property of Thomas Prosser in His Trial on 11 September 1800*. Library of Virginia, Richmond. http://www.lva.virginia.org/whoweare/exhibits/DeathLiberty/gabriel/evidence.htm.

———. *Executive Papers of Governor James Monroe, 1799–1802*.

———. *Proceedings of a Court of Oyer and Terminer in Henrico County*. Library of Virginia, Richmond. http://www.lva.virginia.org/whoweare/exhibits/DeathLiberty/gabriel/oyer18.htm.

———. *Testimony in the Trial of Gabriel*. 1800. Library of Virginia, Richmond. http://www.lva.virginia.org/whoweare/exhibits/DeathLiberty/gabriel/gabtrial17.htm.

W., A. Letter to a "Deer Friend." September 20, 1800. Library of Virginia, Richmond. http://www.lva.virginia.org/whoweare/exhibits/DeathLiberty/gabriel/aw13.htm.

BOOKS

Aptheker, Herbert. "Historical Background of the Gabriel Prosser Slave Revolt." In *American Negro Slave Revolts*, 219-26. New York: International, 1974.

Baldwin, James. "Everybody's Protest Novel." In *Notes of a Native Son*, 13-24. Boston: Beacon, 1984.

Berlin, Adele, Marc Zvi Brettler, and Michael Fishbane, eds. *The Jewish Study Bible*. New York: Oxford University Press, 2004.

Berlin, Iva, Marc Favreau, and Steven F. Miller, eds. *Remembering Slavery: African Americans Talk About Their Personal Experiences of Slavery and Emancipation.* New York and Washington, D.C.: New Press/Library of Congress, 1998.

Bondurant, Agnes Meredith. *Poe's Richmond.* Richmond: Garrett & Massie, 1942.

Brana-Shute, Rosemary, and Randy J. Sparks. *Paths to Freedom: Manumission in the Atlantic World.* Columbia: University of South Carolina Press, 2009.

Deans, Bob. *The River Where America Began: A Journey Along the James.* Lanham, MD: Rowman & Littlefield, 2007.

Duke, Maurice. "Impressed on My Childhood, Perhaps on My Imagination: Richmond in the Early 1800s." In *A Richmond Reader, 1733–1983, 33–43.* Chapel Hill: University of North Carolina Press, 1983.

Egerton, Douglas R. *Gabriel's Rebellion: The Virginia Slave Conspiracies of 1800 and 1802.* Chapel Hill: University of North Carolina Press, 1993.

Finseth, Ian Frederick. *Shades of Green: Visions of Nature in the Literature of American Slavery, 1770–1860.* Athens: University of Georgia Press, 2009.

Flournoy, H. W. *Calendar of Virginia State Papers And Other Manuscripts Preserved in the Capitol at Richmond, January 1, 1799, to December 31, 1807.* New York: Kraus, 1890.

Frankel, Benjamin, ed. *History in Dispute. Vol. 13, Saint Dominique Slave Insurrection.* Detroit: St. James, 2003. Gale Group.

"Gabriel Prosser—Life, Gabriel's Rebellion, Impact, Sources." In *Cambridge Encyclopedia*. http://encyclopedia. stateuniversity.com/pages/8132/Gabriel-Prosser.html.

Gill, Harold B. *The Blacksmith in Eighteenth-century Williamsburg: An Account of His Life & Times and of His Craft*. Williamsburg, VA: Colonial Williamsburg, 1977.

Gish, Agnes Evans. *Virginia Taverns, Ordinaries and Coffee Houses: 18th–Early 19th Century Entertainment Along the Buckingham Road*. Westminster, MD: Willow Bend, 2005.

"Haitian Revolution." In *Encyclopedia of African-American Culture and History*. Gale Group.

Hart, Gary. *James Monroe*. New York: Times Books, 2005.

Hogg, Garry. *Hammer & Tongs: Blacksmithery down the Ages*. London: Hutchison, 1964.

Hurmence, Belinda, ed. *We Lived in a Little Cabin in the Yard*. Winston-Salem, NC: John E. Blair, 1994.

Isaac, Rhys. *Landon Carter's Uneasy Kingdom: Revolution and Rebellion on a Virginia Plantation*. New York: Oxford University Press, 2004.

Jacobs, Jane. *The Death and Life of Great American Cities*. New York: Pelican, 1964.

Jones, Edward P. *The Known World: A Novel*. New York: Harper, 2004.

Jones, Jacqueline. *Labor of Love, Labor of Sorrow: Black Women, Work, and the Family from Slavery to the Present*. New York: Basic, 1985.

Katz, William Loren, ed. *The American Negro: His History and Literature*. New York: Arno Press/New York Times, 1968.

Kimball, Fiske. *The Capitol of Virginia: A Landmark of American Architecture*. Richmond: Virginia State Library and Archives, 1989.

Kukla, Jon. *A Wilderness So Immense: The Louisiana Purchase and the Destiny of America*. New York: Knopf, 2003.

Kulikoff, Allan. *Tobacco and Slaves: The Development of Southern Cultures in the Chesapeake, 1680–1800*. Chapel Hill: University of North Carolina, 1986.

Mack, Angela D., and Stephen G. Hoffius. *Landscape of Slavery: The Plantation in American Art*. Columbia: University of South Carolina Press, 2008.

Marryat, Captain Frederick. *Poor Jack*. London: Longman, Orme, Brown, Green, and Longman, 1840.

Mordecai, Samuel. *Virginia, Especially Richmond, in By-Gone Days*. Richmond: West and Johnson, 1860.

New Jerusalem Bible. Garden City, NJ: Doubleday, 1985.

Pinchbeck, Raymond B. *The Virginia Negro Artisan and Tradesman*. Richmond, VA: William Byrd, 1926.

Richardson, Selden. *Built By Blacks: African American Architecture and Neighborhoods in Richmond, VA*. Richmond: Alliance to Conserve Old Richmond Neighborhoods, 2007.

Rose, Willie Lee. *A Documentary History of Slavery in North America*. New York: Oxford University Press, 1976.

Rucker, Walter C. *The River Flows On: Black Resistance, Culture, and Identity Formation in Early America*. Baton Rouge: Louisiana State University, 2006.

Schwarz, Philip J. *Twice Condemned: Slaves and the Criminal Laws of Virginia, 1705–1865*. Baton Rouge: Louisiana State University, 1988.

———. ed. *Gabriel's Conspiracy: A Documentary History*. Charlottesville: University of Virginia Press, 2012.

Sidbury, James. *Ploughshares Into Swords: Race, Rebellion, and Identity in Gabriel's Virginia, 1730-1810*. New York: Cambridge University Press, 1997.

Smith, Brooks, and Wayne Dementi. *Facts and Legends of the Hills of Richmond*. Manakin-Sabot, VA: Dementi Milestone, 2008.

Styron, William. *The Confessions of Nat Turner*. New York: Random House, 2002.

Tilson, Stephen. *The Role of the Virginia Militia in 1800–1801*. 1974. MS. Virginia Historical Society.

Virginia State Department. *Calendar of Virginia State Papers and Other Manuscripts*. By William Pitt Palmer, Sherwin McRae, Raleigh Colsto, and Henry W. Flournoy. Richmond: R. F. Walker, 1890.

Walsh, Lorena S. *From Calabar to Carter's Grove: The History of a Virginia Slave Community*. Charlottesville: University of Virginia, 1997.

Watson, Aldren Auld. *The Village Blacksmith*. New York: Crowell, 1968.

Weinsfield, Judith. "Nancy Prosser: Biographical Sketch." In *Encyclopedia of African-American Culture and History*. 1996.

Weld, Theodore Dwight. *The Bible Against Slavery, Or,
an Inquiry Into the Genius of the Mosaic System, and the
Teachings of the Old Testament on the Subject of Human Rights.*
Pittsburgh: United Presbyterian Board of Publication, 1864.

Williams, George W. "Excerpt from History of the Negro
Race in America from 1619 to 1880:" 4. Gale Group.

Books for Young Readers

McPherson, Stephanie S. *Sisters Against Slavery: A Story
About Sarah and Angelina Grimké.* Illustrated by Karen
Ritz. Minneapolis: Carolrhoda, 1999.

Siegelson, Kim L. *In the Time of the Drums.* Illustrated by
Brian Pinkney. New York: Jump at the Sun Hyperion,
1999.

Williams, Karen Lynn. *Circles of Hope.* Illustrated by Linda
Saport. Grand Rapids: Eerdmans, 2005.

Articles

Dabney, Virginius. "Gabriel's Insurrection." *American History
Illustrated* 11, no. 4 (1976): 24–32.

DeFord, Susan. "Gabriel's Rebellion." *Washington Post,*
February 26, 2000.

Durkin, Anita. "Object Written, Written Object: Slavery,
Scarring, and Complications of Authorship in *Beloved.*"
African American Review 41, no. 3 (fall 2007): 541–56.

"Gabriel's Insurrection." *Henrico County Historical Society
Magazine,* Fall 1979.

"Gabriel's Rebellion in Henrico County." *Henrico County Historical Society Newsletter* 3, no. 1 (1996), 13 November 1996.

"Haiti Gains Its Independence, 1804." *Discovering World History*. Online Edition. Farmington Hills, MI (2003).

Higginson, T. W. "Gabriel's Defeat." *Atlantic Monthly*, vol. X, Boston: Ticknor and Fields (1862), 337–345.

Hinks, Peter P. "Gabriel's Rebellion." *Magill's Literary Annual* (1994). *ENotes*. http://www.enotes.com/gabriels-rebellion-salem/gabriels-rebellion.

Kelly, Deborah. "Slave Got His Day in New Park." *Richmond Times Dispatch*, August 31, 1997.

Schwarz, Philip J. "Gabriel's Challenge: Slaves and Crime in the Late Eighteenth-Century Virginia." *Virginia Magazine of History and Biography* 90, no. 3 (1982), 283–309.

Slipek, Edwin. "Monroe's Legacy: Soldier, Founding Father, President. Richmond's Connection to the Man Who Served in More Exulted Positions Than Any Other American — Ever." *Style Weekly*, April 16, 2008: 14+.

Tragle, Henry Irving. "Styron and His Sources." *Massachusetts Review* 11, no. 1 (1970).

Veney, Cassandra. "Nancy Prosser: Biographical Sketch." *African American National Biography* 6 (2008): 459–60.

Weiss, John. "The Horrors of San Domingo." *Atlantic Monthly*, vol. X, Boston: Ticknor and Fields (1862), 347–358.

Dementi, Wayne, and Brooks Smith. "Facts and Legends of the Hills of Richmond." Lecture, April 8, 2009. Virginia Center for Architecture, Richmond.

Gordon-Reed, Annette. "A Lens on American Cultural History: A Conversation with Annette Gordon-Reed." Lecture, October 17, 2009. Library of Virginia Literary Luncheon, Richmond, Virginia.

Khout, Ken. Introduction to Blacksmithing, June 2009. The Visual Arts Center, Richmond.

Lee, Lauranett L. "Sites and Stories: African American History in Virginia." Lecture, May 5, 2009. Virginia Historical Society, Richmond. http://www.vahistorical.org/news/lectures_lee.htm.

Mann, Charles C. "Tobacco, Mosquito, Slave: Colonial Virginia and the Dawn of Globalization." Lecture, April 30, 2009. Virginia Historical Society, Richmond. http://www.vahistorical.org/news/lectures_lumpkins.htm.

Ruggle, Jeffery. "Shockoe Valley Topography and the Slave Trade." Lecture, April 30, 2009. Virginia Historical Society, Richmond. http://www.vahistorical.org/news/lectures_lumpkins.htm.

Sharpe, Jay. Forged bracelets and metal jewelry viewed by the author, June 2010. The Visual Arts Center, Richmond, VA.

Interviews

Edwards, Ana, chair, Sacred Ground Historical Reclamation Project. Interview with the author, June 10, 2009.

Kukla, Jon, former director of historical research, Library of Virginia. Interview with the author, discussing Richmond in the 1800s, February 25, 2010.

Sanderson, John W., Sr., family farmer. Interview with the author, discussing tobacco farming, June 6, 2009.

Swenson, Kristin, author of *Bible Babel: Making Sense of the Most Talked About Book of All Time*. Interview with the author, discussing the Book of Daniel, February 12, 2010.

Audiovisual Resources

The Trades of Colonial Williamsburg: Hammerman in Williamsburg. The Colonial Williamsburg Foundation, 1973. DVD.

ACKNOWLEDGMENTS

Thank you to Dr. Philip J. Schwarz, who shared his manuscript, *Gabriel's Rebellion, 1800: A Documentary History*, published in December 2012 by the University of Virginia Press. Historian Jon Kukla kindly helped me better understand concepts such as maternal descent, manumission, and early American currency. Biblical scholar Kristin Swenson helped me consider the Bible differently. My sister, Leigh Amateau, and her friend Janet Monclure arranged for me to visit the historic Tinsley family farm in Hanover County. More than anything else, the day I spent at Topotomoi enlivened this story. Thank you to the librarians at the Bon Air Branch of Chesterfield County Public Library, the Library of Virginia, and the Virginia Historical Society. Thanks to my early readers and great thinkers: Judith Amateau, Ana Edwards, Reggie Gordon, Mary Ellis Gregg, Mary Kiger, Meg Medina, Nylce Prada Myers, Nancy Rives, Bubba Sanderson, Emily Sanderson, and Amy Strite. Thank you to my kind, insightful, and really smart agent, Leigh Feldman of Writers House. Thank you, Candlewick Press, for your encouragement and excellent support. My awesome family — I need much more space to thank you properly.

Most especially, thank you, Karen Lotz, for your guidance, wisdom, and beautiful heart. And for crouching within the door with me, close enough to catch the first spark of this book by candlelight at Mount Vernon. The most gratitude of all is owed to Gabriel, the boys on the brook, and to Gabriel's Nan for believing in the business of liberty and insisting upon it.